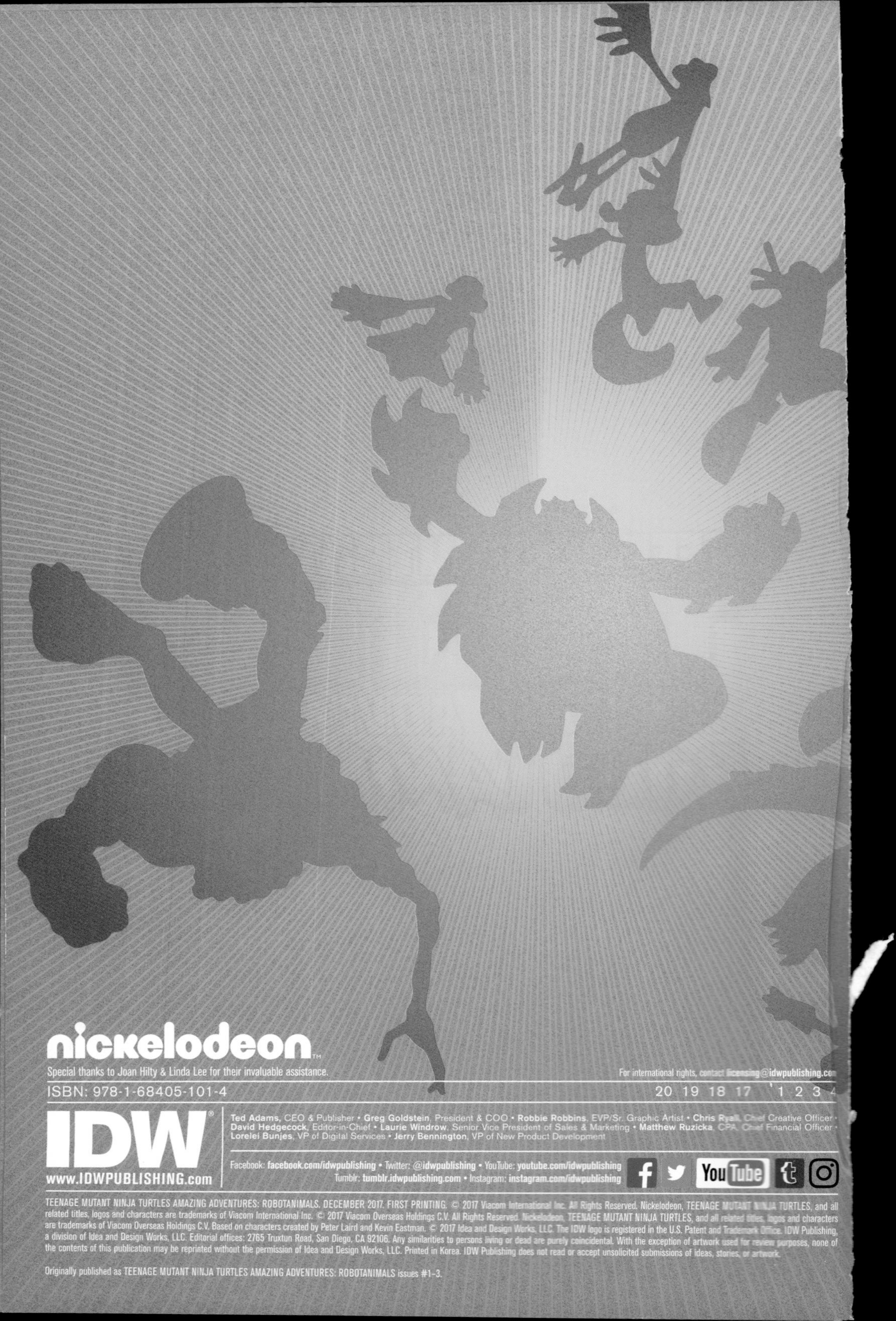

Special thanks to Joan Hilty & Linda Lee for their invaluable assistance.

For international rights, contact licensing@idwpublishing.com

ISBN: 978-1-68405-101-4

20 19 18 17 1 2 3 4

Ted Adams, CEO & Publisher • **Greg Goldstein**, President & COO • **Robbie Robbins**, EVP/Sr. Graphic Artist • **Chris Ryall**, Chief Creative Officer • **David Hedgecock**, Editor-in-Chief • **Laurie Windrow**, Senior Vice President of Sales & Marketing • **Matthew Ruzicka**, CPA, Chief Financial Officer • **Lorelei Bunjes**, VP of Digital Services • **Jerry Bennington**, VP of New Product Development

www.IDWPUBLISHING.com

Facebook: **facebook.com/idwpublishing** • Twitter: **@idwpublishing** • YouTube: **youtube.com/idwpublishing**
Tumblr: **tumblr.idwpublishing.com** • Instagram: **instagram.com/idwpublishing**

Originally published as TEENAGE MUTANT NINJA TURTLES AMAZING ADVENTURES: ROBOTANIMALS issues #1–3.

Writer: Caleb Goellner
Artist: Chad Thomas
Colorist: Heather Breckel
Letterers: Shawn Lee & Christa Miesner
Series Editors: Peter Adrian Behravesh & Bobby Curnow

Cover Artist: Chad Thomas
Collection Editors: Justin Eisinger & Alonzo Simon
Collection Designer: Shawn Lee
Publisher: Ted Adams

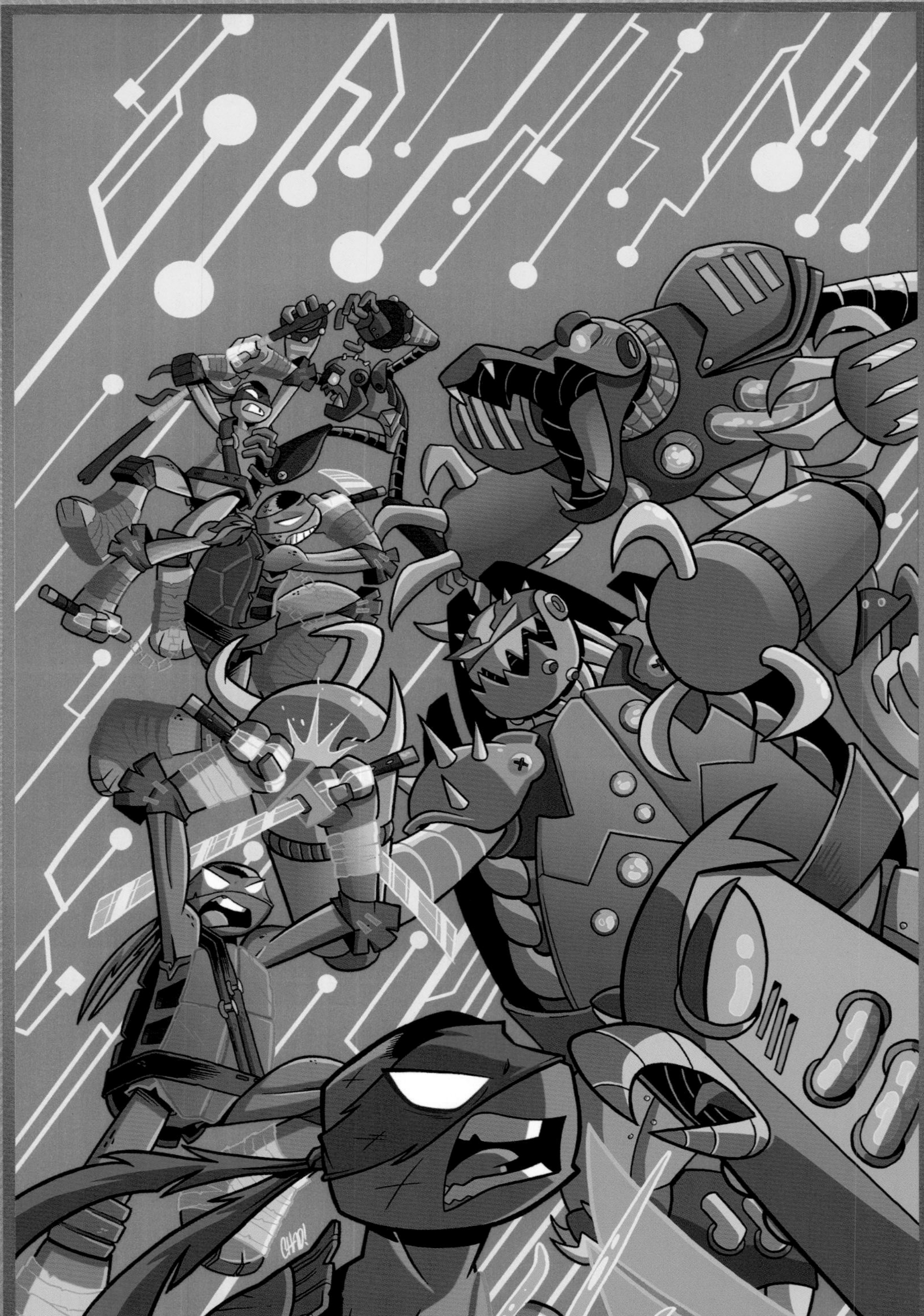
CHAD!

Artist: Chad Thomas

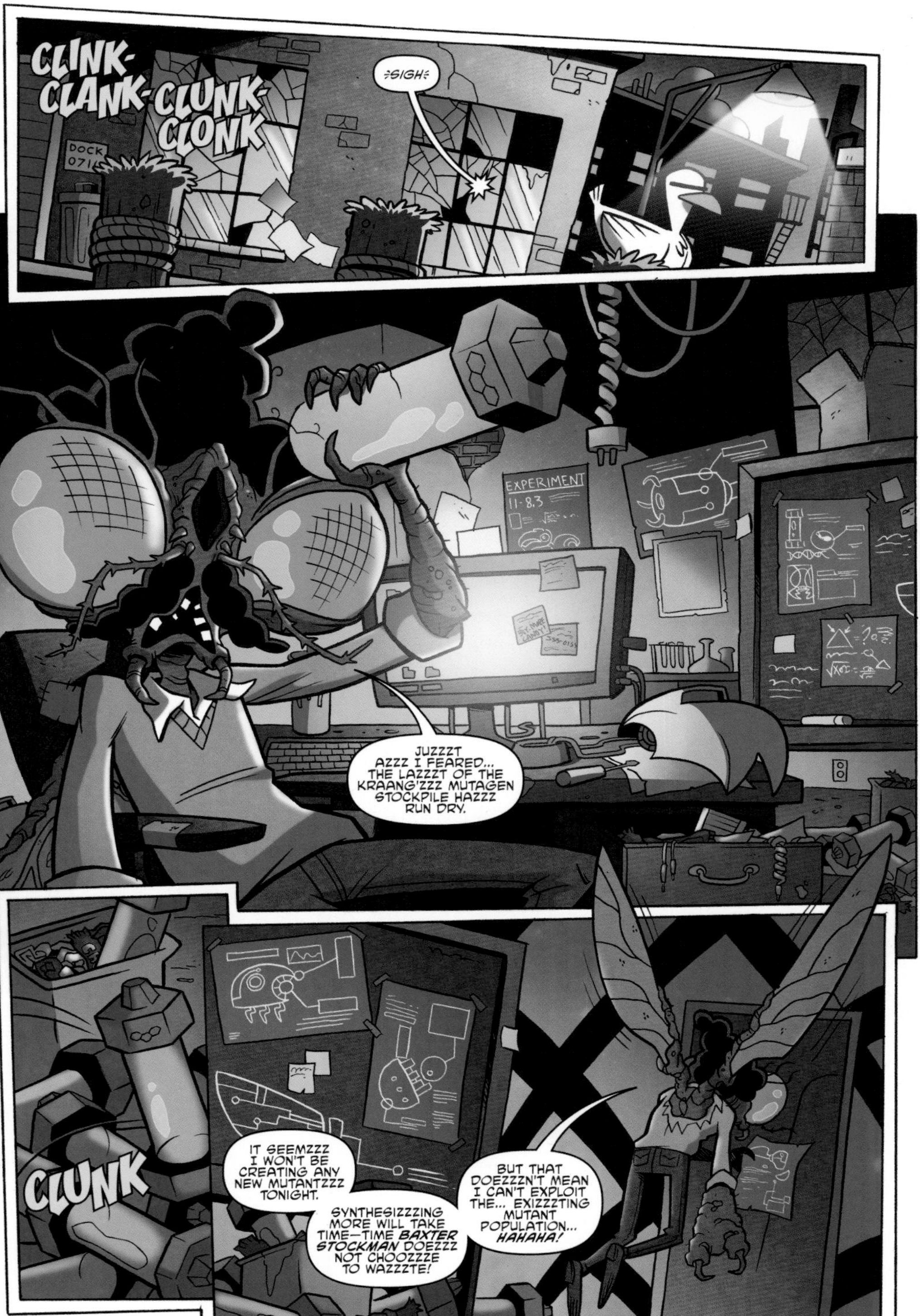

CLINK-
CLANK-
CLUNK-
CLONK
DOCK 071
SIGH
EXPERIMENT 11-8.3
JUZZZT AZZZ I FEARED... THE LAZZZT OF THE KRAANG'ZZZ MUTAGEN STOCKPILE HAZZZ RUN DRY.
CLUNK
IT SEEMZZZ I WON'T BE CREATING ANY NEW MUTANTZZZZ TONIGHT.
SYNTHESIZZZING MORE WILL TAKE TIME—TIME BAXTER STOCKMAN DOEZZZ NOT CHOOZZZE TO WAZZZTE!
BUT THAT DOEZZZN'T MEAN I CAN'T EXPLOIT THE... EXIZZZTING MUTANT POPULATION... HAHAHA!

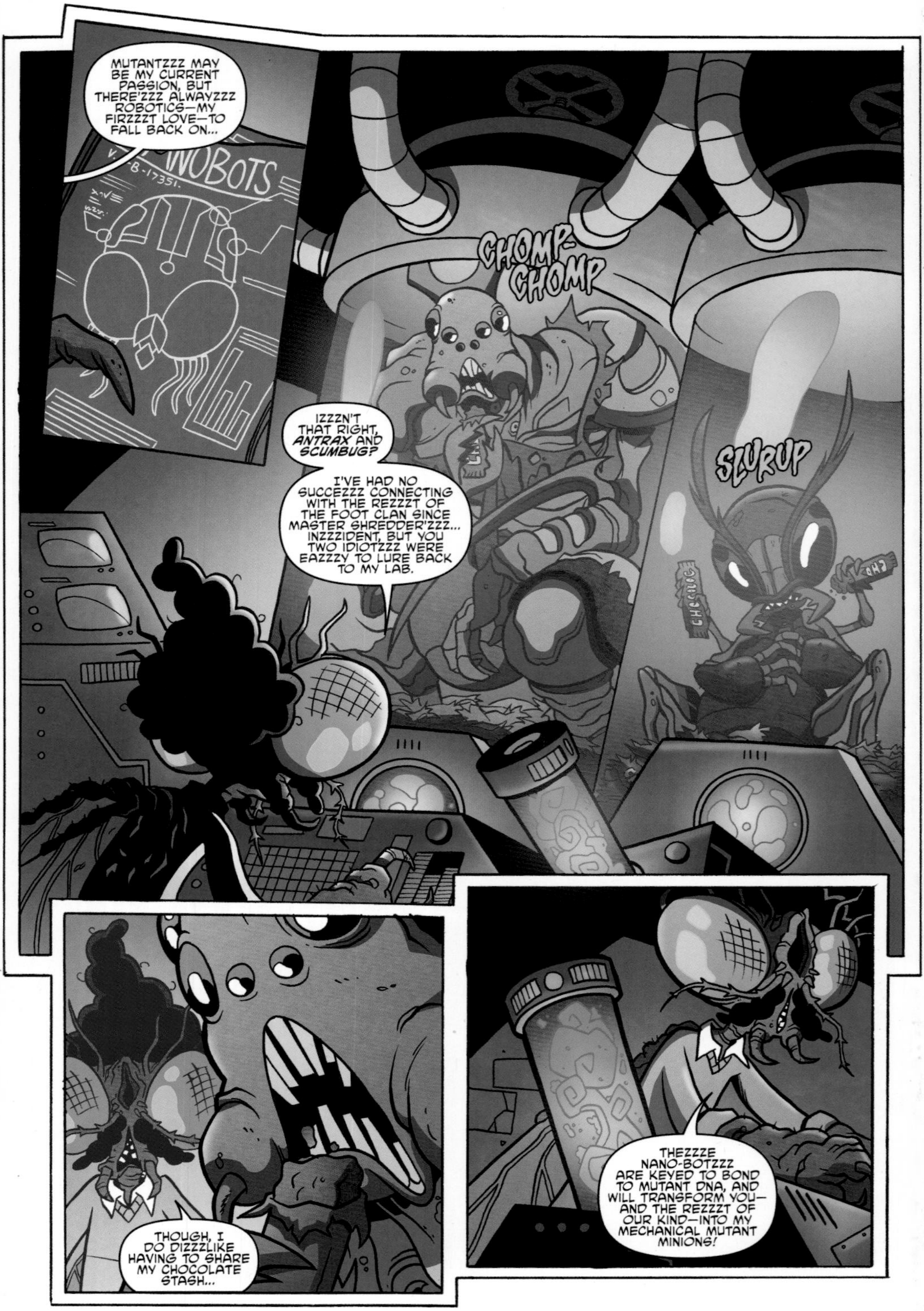

MUTANTZZZ MAY BE MY CURRENT PASSION, BUT THERE'ZZZ ALWAYZZZ ROBOTICS—MY FIRZZZT LOVE—TO FALL BACK ON...
CHOMP-CHOMP
IZZZN'T THAT RIGHT, *ANTRAX* AND *SCUMBUG*?
SLURUP
I'VE HAD NO SUCCEZZZ CONNECTING WITH THE REZZZT OF THE FOOT CLAN SINCE MASTER SHREDDER'ZZZ... INZZZIDENT, BUT YOU TWO IDIOTZZZ WERE EAZZZY TO LURE BACK TO MY LAB.
THOUGH, I DO DIZZZLIKE HAVING TO SHARE MY CHOCOLATE STASH...
THEZZZE NANO-BOTZZZ ARE KEYED TO BOND TO MUTANT DNA, AND WILL TRANSFORM YOU—AND THE REZZZT OF OUR KIND—INTO MY MECHANICAL MUTANT MINIONS!

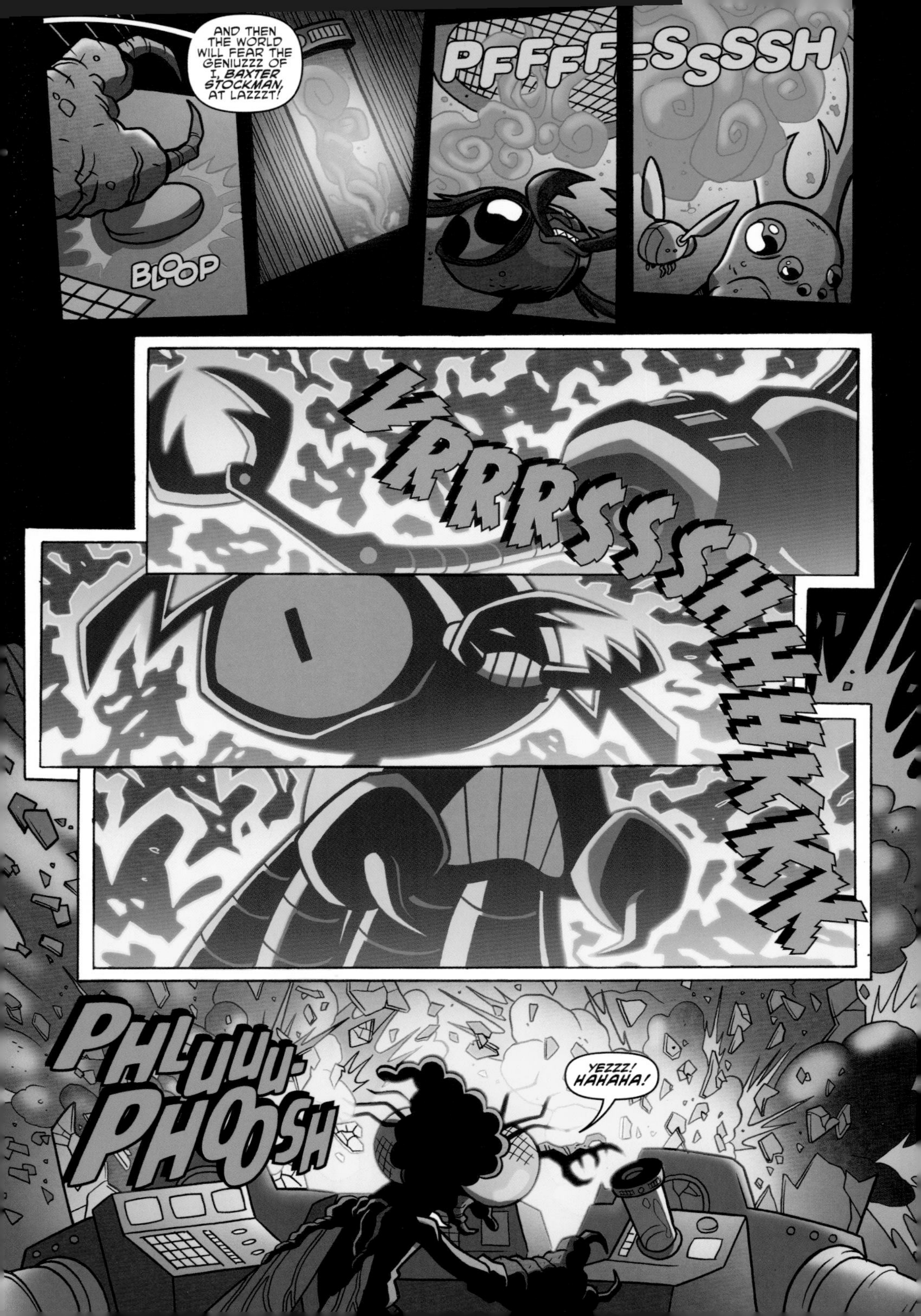
AND THEN THE WORLD WILL FEAR THE GENIUZZZ OF I, BAXTER STOCKMAN, AT LAZZZT!
BLOOP
PFFFFF-SSSSSH
VRRRSSSSHHHKKKK
PHLUUU-PHOOSH
YEZZZ! HAHAHA!

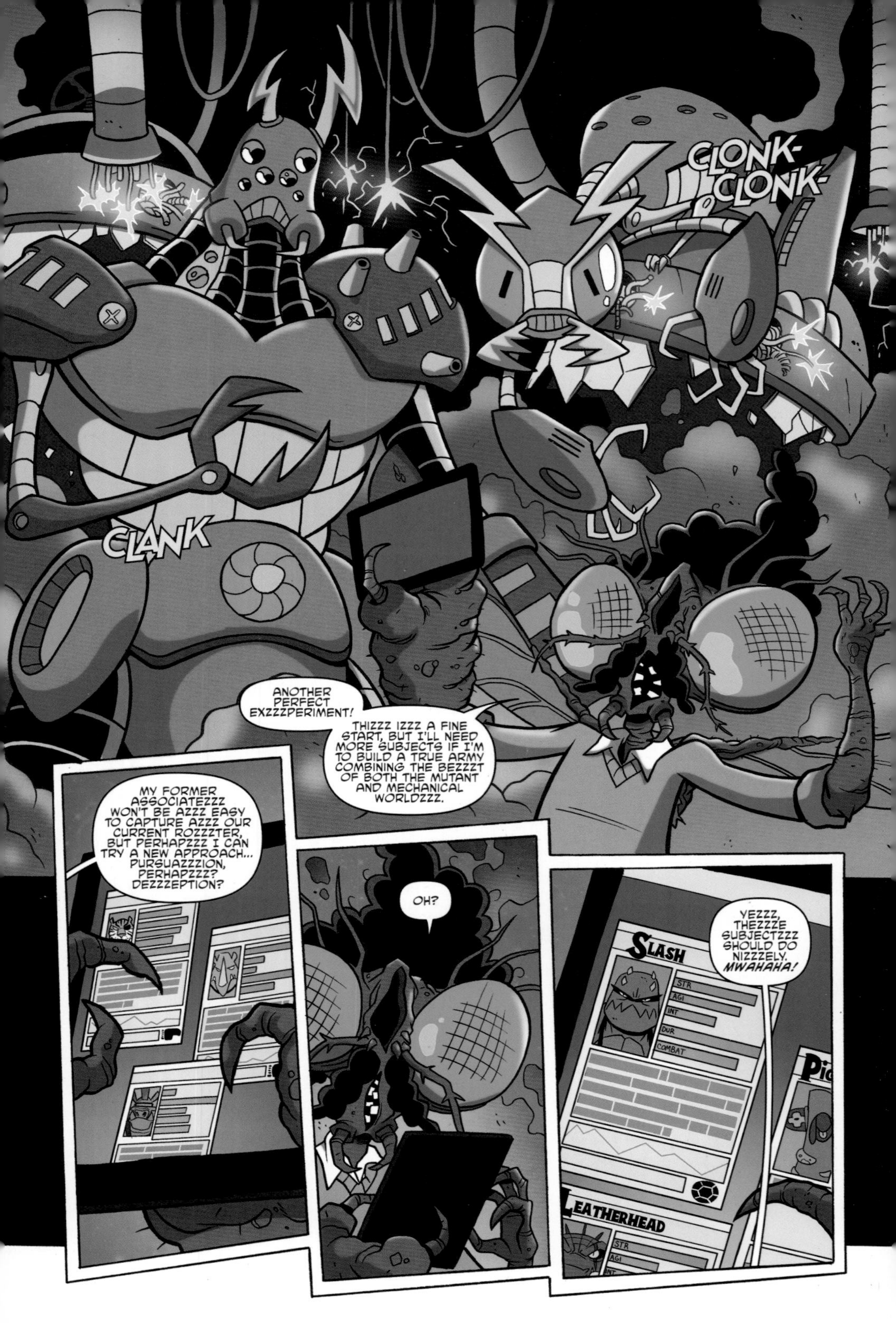
CLONK-
CLONK-
CLANK
ANOTHER PERFECT EXZZZPERIMENT!
THIZZZ IZZZ A FINE START, BUT I'LL NEED MORE SUBJECTS IF I'M TO BUILD A TRUE ARMY COMBINING THE BEZZZT OF BOTH THE MUTANT AND MECHANICAL WORLDZZZ.
MY FORMER ASSOCIATEZZZ WON'T BE AZZZ EASY TO CAPTURE AZZZ OUR CURRENT ROZZZTER, BUT PERHAPZZZ I CAN TRY A NEW APPROACH... PURSUAZZZION, PERHAPZZZ? DEZZZEPTION?
OH?
YEZZZ, THEZZZE SUBJECTZZZ SHOULD DO NIZZZELY. MWAHAHA!
SLASH
STR
AGI
INT
DUR
COMBAT
LEATHERHEAD
STR
AGI

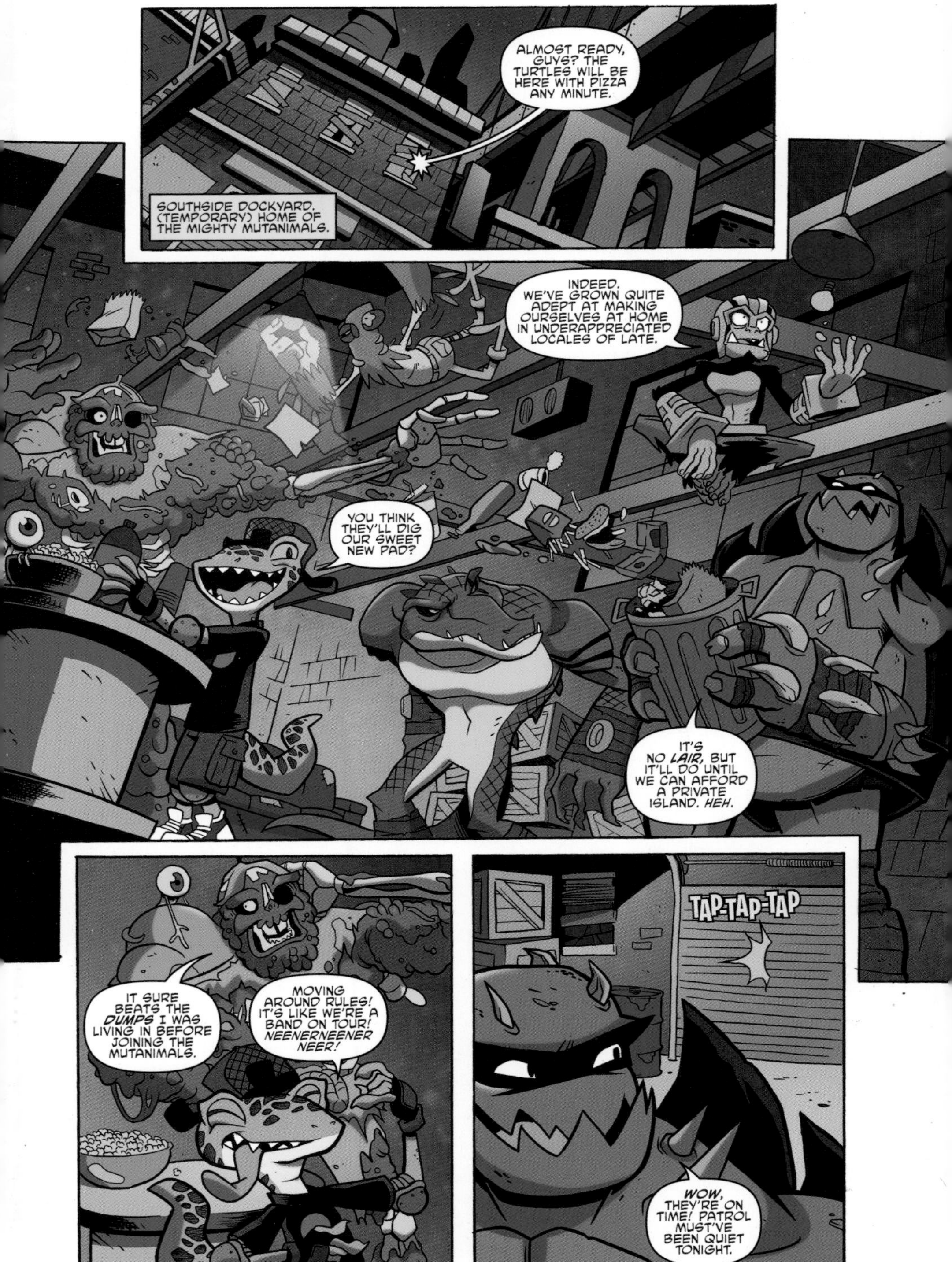

SOUTHSIDE DOCKYARD. (TEMPORARY) HOME OF THE MIGHTY MUTANIMALS.
ALMOST READY, GUYS? THE TURTLES WILL BE HERE WITH PIZZA ANY MINUTE.
INDEED. WE'VE GROWN QUITE ADEPT AT MAKING OURSELVES AT HOME IN UNDERAPPRECIATED LOCALES OF LATE.
YOU THINK THEY'LL DIG OUR SWEET NEW PAD?
IT'S NO *LAIR*, BUT IT'LL DO UNTIL WE CAN AFFORD A PRIVATE ISLAND. *HEH.*
IT SURE BEATS THE *DUMPS* I WAS LIVING IN BEFORE JOINING THE MUTANIMALS.
MOVING AROUND RULES! IT'S LIKE WE'RE A BAND ON TOUR! *NEENERNEENER NEER!*
TAP-TAP-TAP
WOW, THEY'RE ON TIME! PATROL MUST'VE BEEN QUIET TONIGHT.

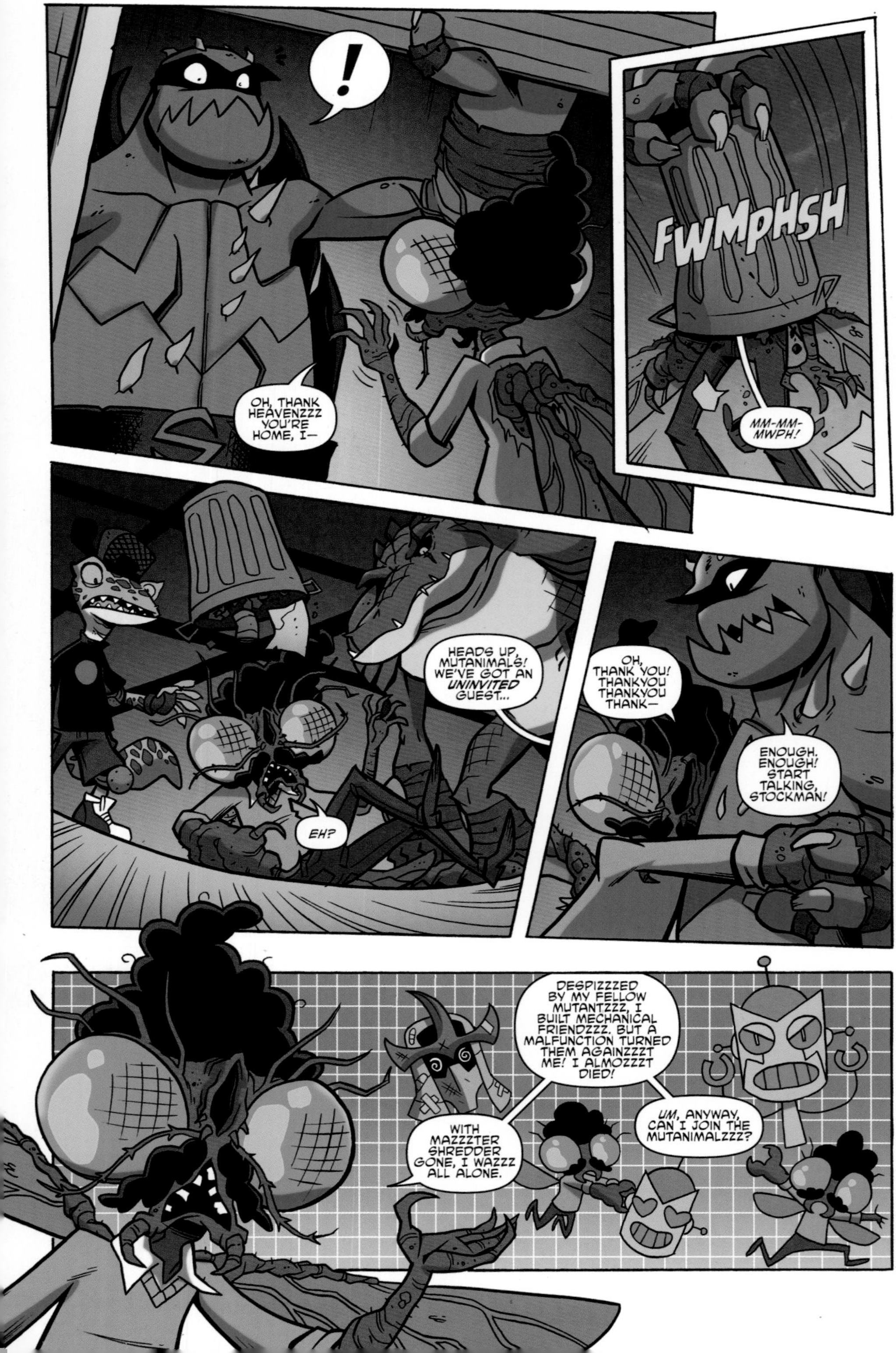
!
OH, THANK HEAVENZZZ YOU'RE HOME, I—
FWMPHSH
MM-MM-MWPH!
HEADS UP, MUTANIMALS! WE'VE GOT AN *UNINVITED* GUEST...
EH?
OH, THANK YOU! THANKYOU THANKYOU THANK—
ENOUGH. ENOUGH! START TALKING, STOCKMAN!
WITH MAZZZTER SHREDDER GONE, I WAZZZ ALL ALONE.
DESPIZZZED BY MY FELLOW MUTANTZZZ, I BUILT MECHANICAL FRIENDZZZ. BUT A MALFUNCTION TURNED THEM AGAINZZZT ME! I ALMOZZZT DIED!
UM, ANYWAY, CAN I JOIN THE MUTANIMALZZZ?

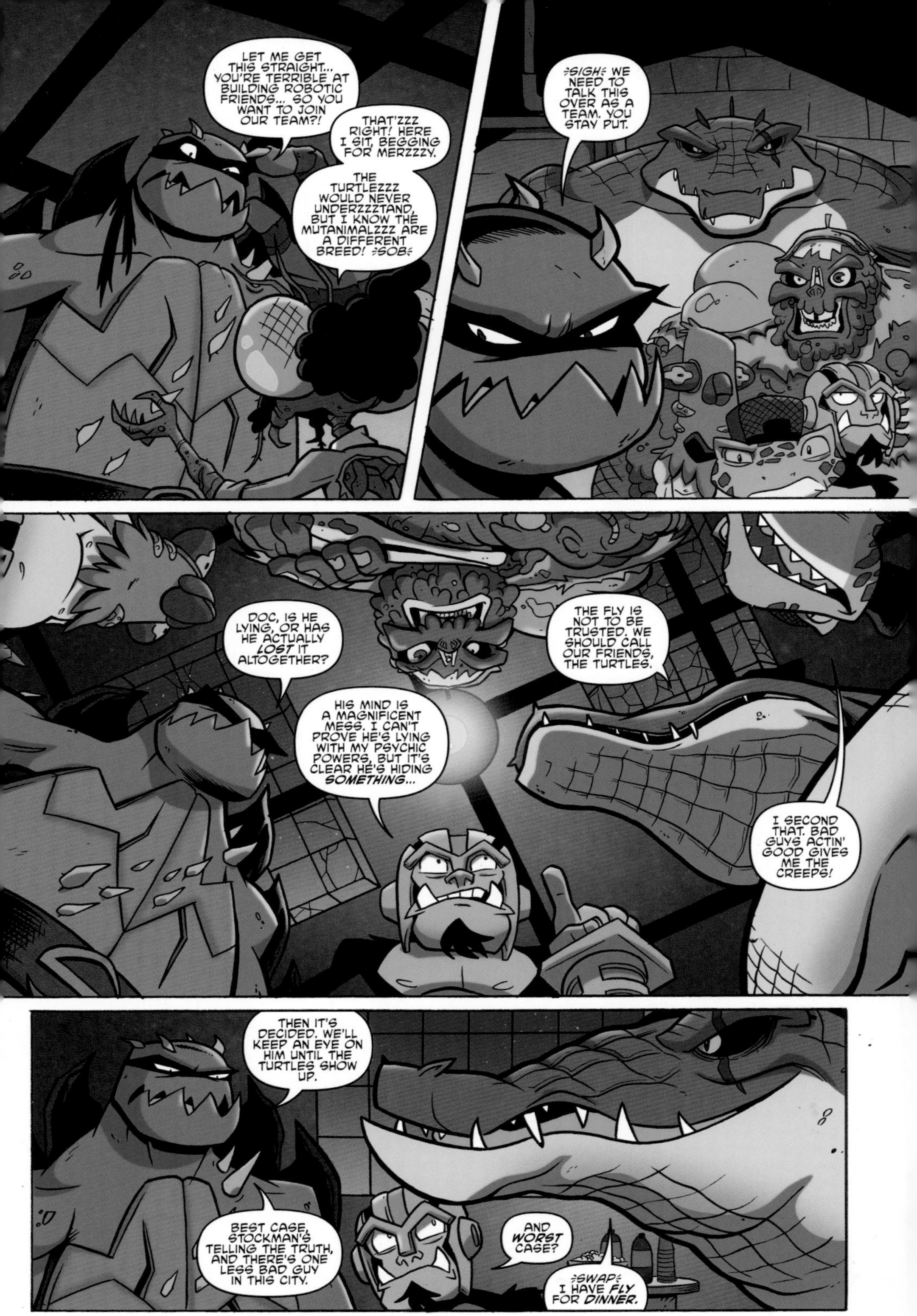
LET ME GET THIS STRAIGHT... YOU'RE TERRIBLE AT BUILDING ROBOTIC FRIENDS... SO YOU WANT TO JOIN OUR TEAM?!
THAT'ZZZ RIGHT! HERE I SIT, BEGGING FOR MERZZZY.
THE TURTLEZZZ WOULD NEVER UNDERZZZTAND, BUT I KNOW THE MUTANIMALZZZ ARE A DIFFERENT BREED! ⸗SOB⸗
⸗SIGH⸗ WE NEED TO TALK THIS OVER AS A TEAM. YOU STAY PUT.
DOC, IS HE LYING, OR HAS HE ACTUALLY *LOST* IT ALTOGETHER?
HIS MIND IS A MAGNIFICENT MESS. I CAN'T PROVE HE'S LYING WITH MY PSYCHIC POWERS, BUT IT'S CLEAR HE'S HIDING ***SOMETHING***...
THE FLY IS NOT TO BE TRUSTED. WE SHOULD CALL OUR FRIENDS, THE TURTLES.
I SECOND THAT. BAD GUYS ACTIN' GOOD GIVES ME THE CREEPS!
THEN IT'S DECIDED. WE'LL KEEP AN EYE ON HIM UNTIL THE TURTLES SHOW UP.
BEST CASE, STOCKMAN'S TELLING THE TRUTH, AND THERE'S ONE LESS BAD GUY IN THIS CITY.
AND ***WORST*** CASE?
⸗SWAP⸗ I HAVE ***FLY*** FOR ***DINNER.***

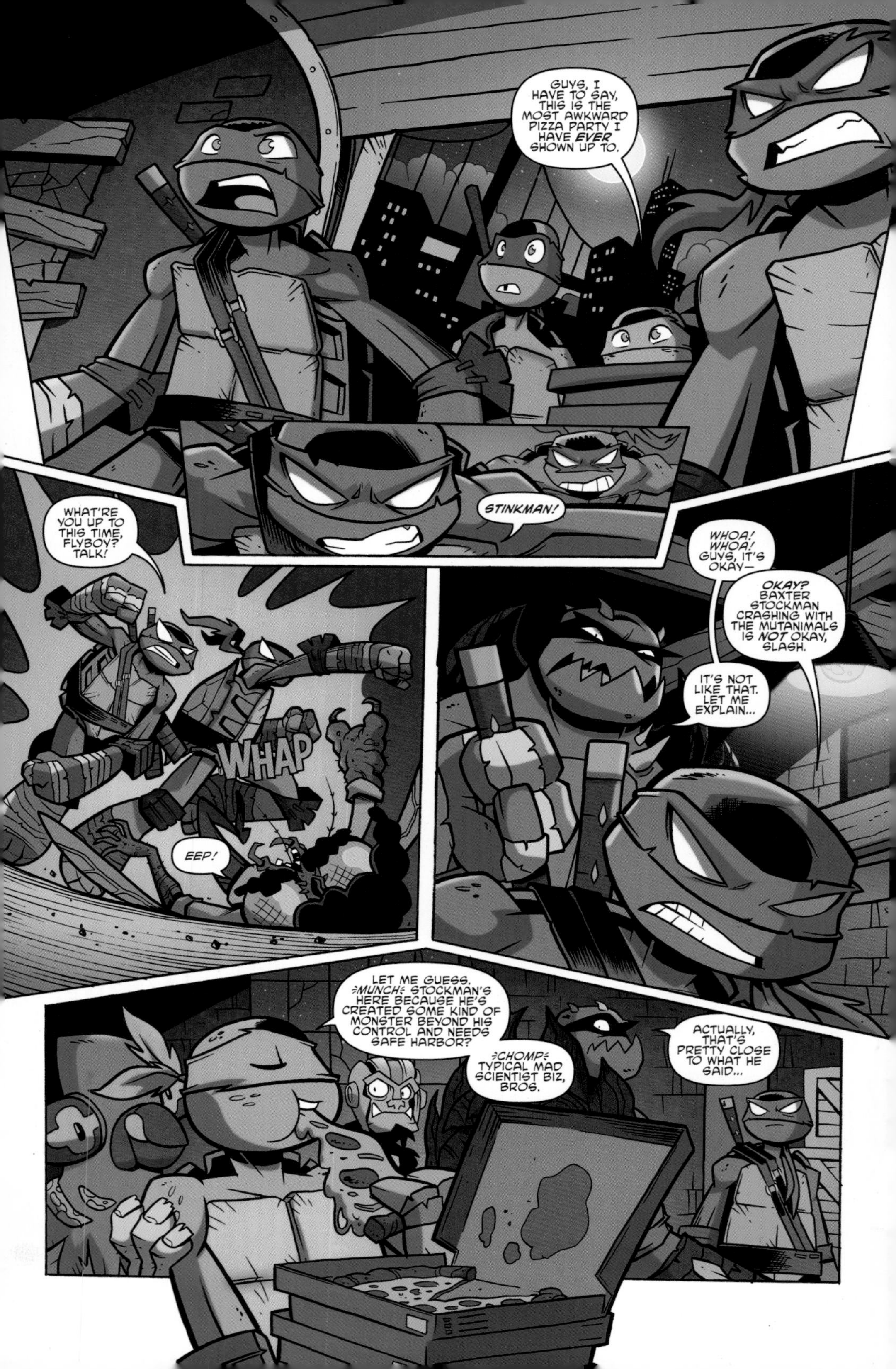
GUYS, I HAVE TO SAY, THIS IS THE MOST AWKWARD PIZZA PARTY I HAVE EVER SHOWN UP TO.
STINKMAN!
WHAT'RE YOU UP TO THIS TIME, FLYBOY? TALK!
WHAP
EEP!
WHOA! WHOA! GUYS, IT'S OKAY—
OKAY? BAXTER STOCKMAN CRASHING WITH THE MUTANIMALS IS NOT OKAY, SLASH.
IT'S NOT LIKE THAT. LET ME EXPLAIN...
LET ME GUESS. MUNCH STOCKMAN'S HERE BECAUSE HE'S CREATED SOME KIND OF MONSTER BEYOND HIS CONTROL AND NEEDS SAFE HARBOR?
CHOMP TYPICAL MAD SCIENTIST BIZ, BROS.
ACTUALLY, THAT'S PRETTY CLOSE TO WHAT HE SAID...

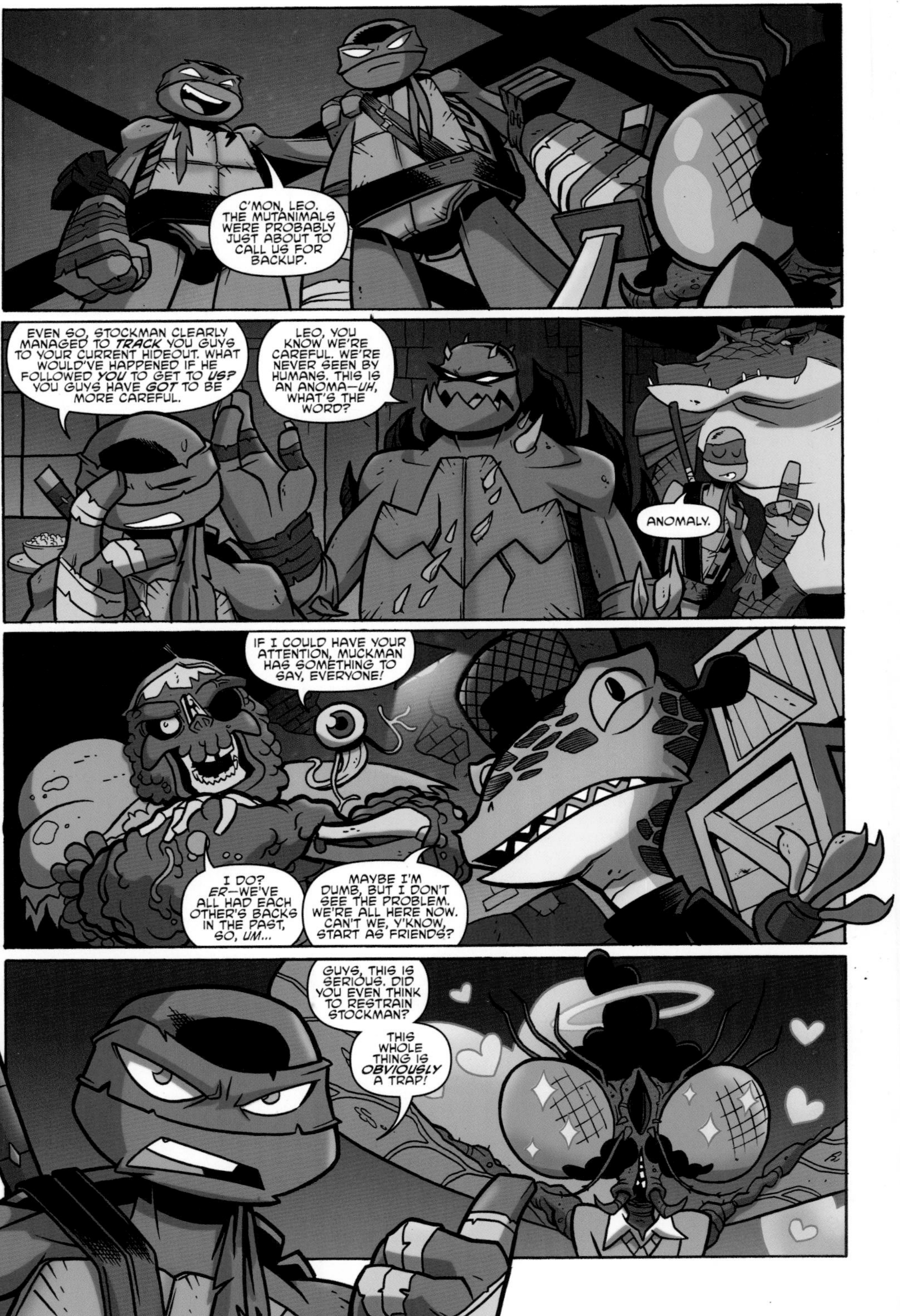
C'MON, LEO. THE MUTANIMALS WERE PROBABLY JUST ABOUT TO CALL US FOR BACKUP.
EVEN SO, STOCKMAN CLEARLY MANAGED TO *TRACK* YOU GUYS TO YOUR CURRENT HIDEOUT. WHAT WOULD'VE HAPPENED IF HE FOLLOWED *YOU* TO GET TO *US?* YOU GUYS HAVE *GOT* TO BE MORE CAREFUL.
LEO, YOU KNOW WE'RE CAREFUL. WE'RE NEVER SEEN BY HUMANS. THIS IS AN ANOMA—*UH*, WHAT'S THE WORD?
ANOMALY.
IF I COULD HAVE YOUR ATTENTION, MUCKMAN HAS SOMETHING TO SAY, EVERYONE!
I DO? *ER*—WE'VE ALL HAD EACH OTHER'S BACKS IN THE PAST, SO, *UM*...
MAYBE I'M DUMB, BUT I DON'T SEE THE PROBLEM. WE'RE ALL HERE NOW. CAN'T WE, Y'KNOW, START AS FRIENDS?
GUYS, THIS IS SERIOUS. DID YOU EVEN THINK TO RESTRAIN STOCKMAN?
THIS WHOLE THING IS *OBVIOUSLY* A TRAP!

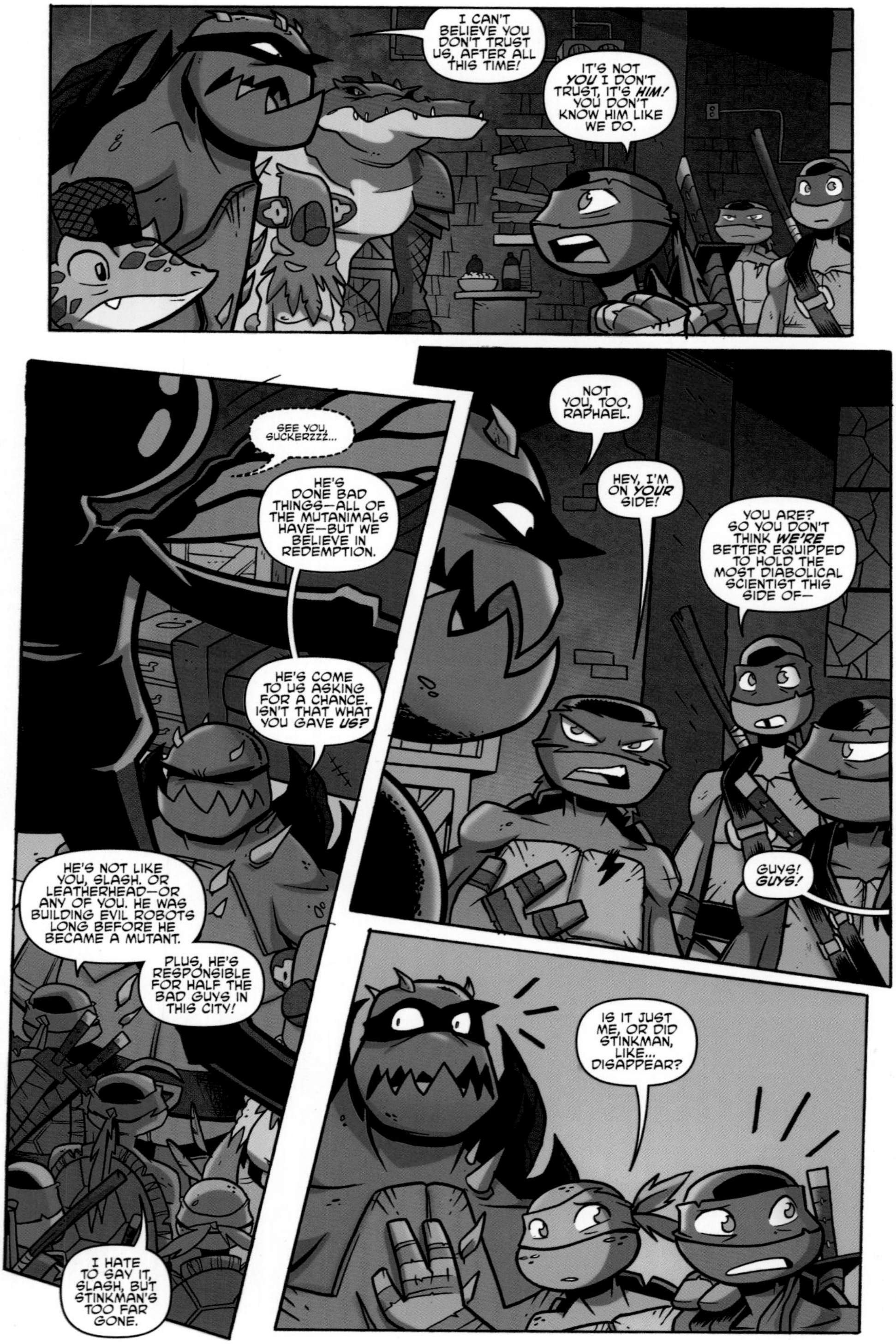
I CAN'T BELIEVE YOU DON'T TRUST US, AFTER ALL THIS TIME!
IT'S NOT *YOU* I DON'T TRUST, IT'S *HIM!* YOU DON'T KNOW HIM LIKE WE DO.
SEE YOU, SUCKERZZZ...
HE'S DONE BAD THINGS—ALL OF THE MUTANIMALS HAVE—BUT WE BELIEVE IN REDEMPTION.
HE'S COME TO US ASKING FOR A CHANCE. ISN'T THAT WHAT YOU GAVE *US?*
HE'S NOT LIKE YOU, SLASH. OR LEATHERHEAD—OR ANY OF YOU. HE WAS BUILDING EVIL ROBOTS LONG BEFORE HE BECAME A MUTANT.
PLUS, HE'S RESPONSIBLE FOR HALF THE BAD GUYS IN THIS CITY!
I HATE TO SAY IT, SLASH, BUT STINKMAN'S TOO FAR GONE.
NOT YOU, TOO, RAPHAEL.
HEY, I'M ON *YOUR* SIDE!
YOU ARE? SO YOU DON'T THINK *WE'RE* BETTER EQUIPPED TO HOLD THE MOST DIABOLICAL SCIENTIST THIS SIDE OF—
GUYS! *GUYS!*
IS IT JUST ME, OR DID STINKMAN, LIKE... DISAPPEAR?

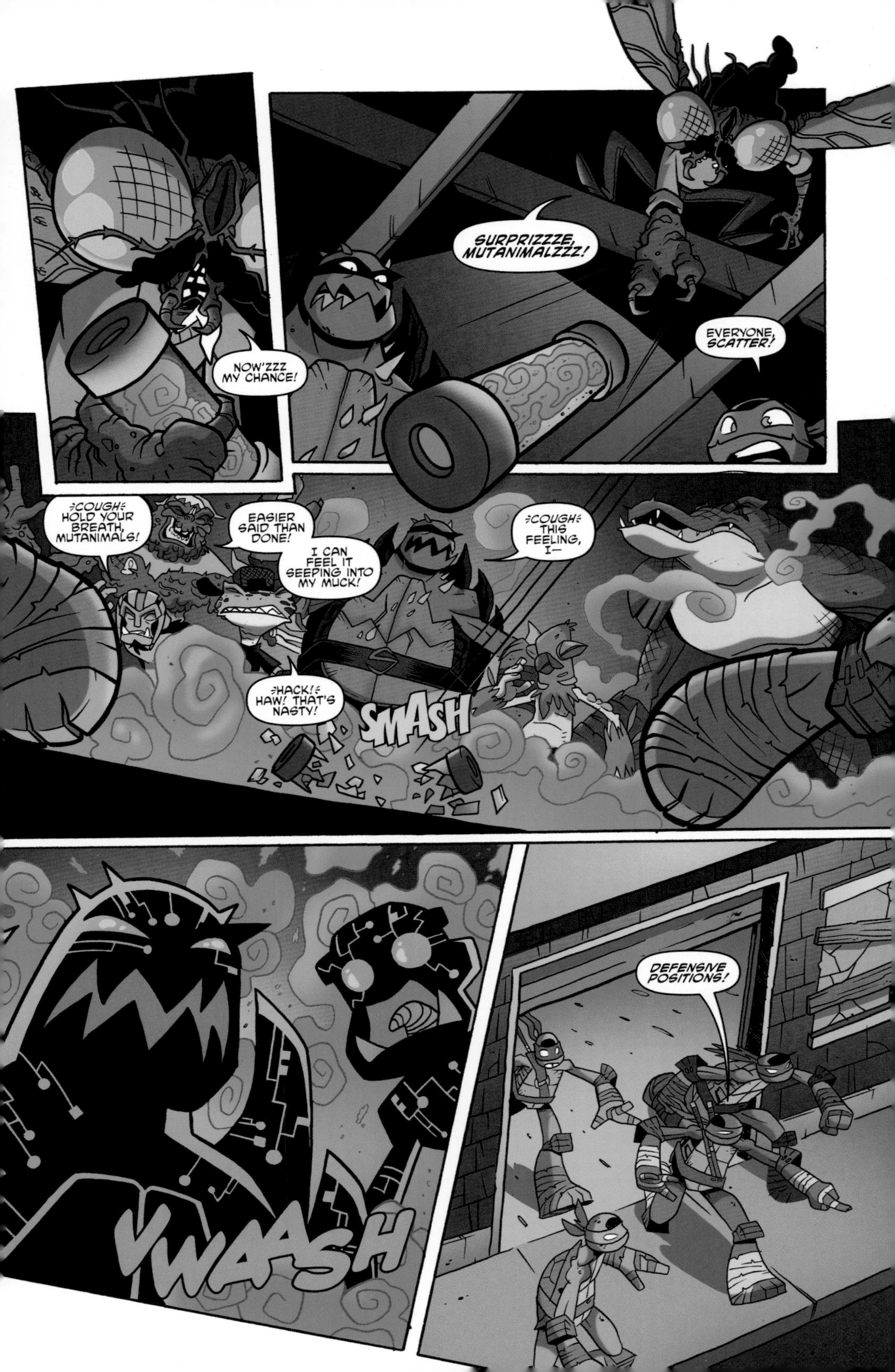
SURPRIZZZE, MUTANIMALZZZ!
NOW'ZZZ MY CHANCE!
EVERYONE, SCATTER!
COUGH HOLD YOUR BREATH, MUTANIMALS!
EASIER SAID THAN DONE!
I CAN FEEL IT SEEPING INTO MY MUCK!
COUGH THIS FEELING, I—
HACK! HAW! THAT'S NASTY!
SMASH
VWASH
DEFENSIVE POSITIONS!

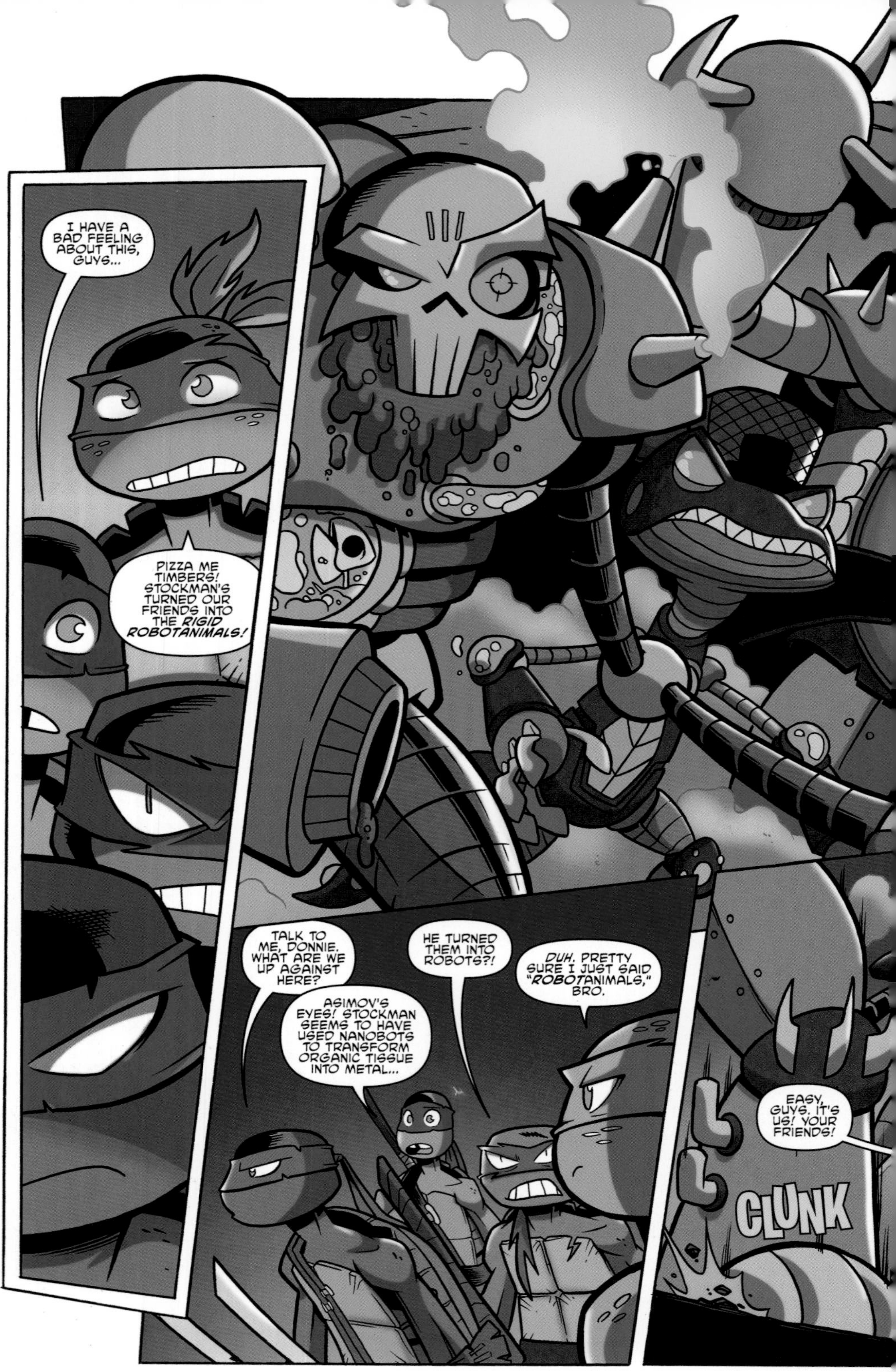
I HAVE A BAD FEELING ABOUT THIS, GUYS...
PIZZA ME TIMBERS! STOCKMAN'S TURNED OUR FRIENDS INTO THE *RIGID ROBOTANIMALS!*
TALK TO ME, DONNIE. WHAT ARE WE UP AGAINST HERE?
ASIMOV'S EYES! STOCKMAN SEEMS TO HAVE USED NANOBOTS TO TRANSFORM ORGANIC TISSUE INTO METAL...
HE TURNED THEM INTO ROBOTS?!
DUH. PRETTY SURE I JUST SAID "*ROBOT*ANIMALS," BRO.
EASY, GUYS. IT'S *US!* YOUR FRIENDS!
CLUNK

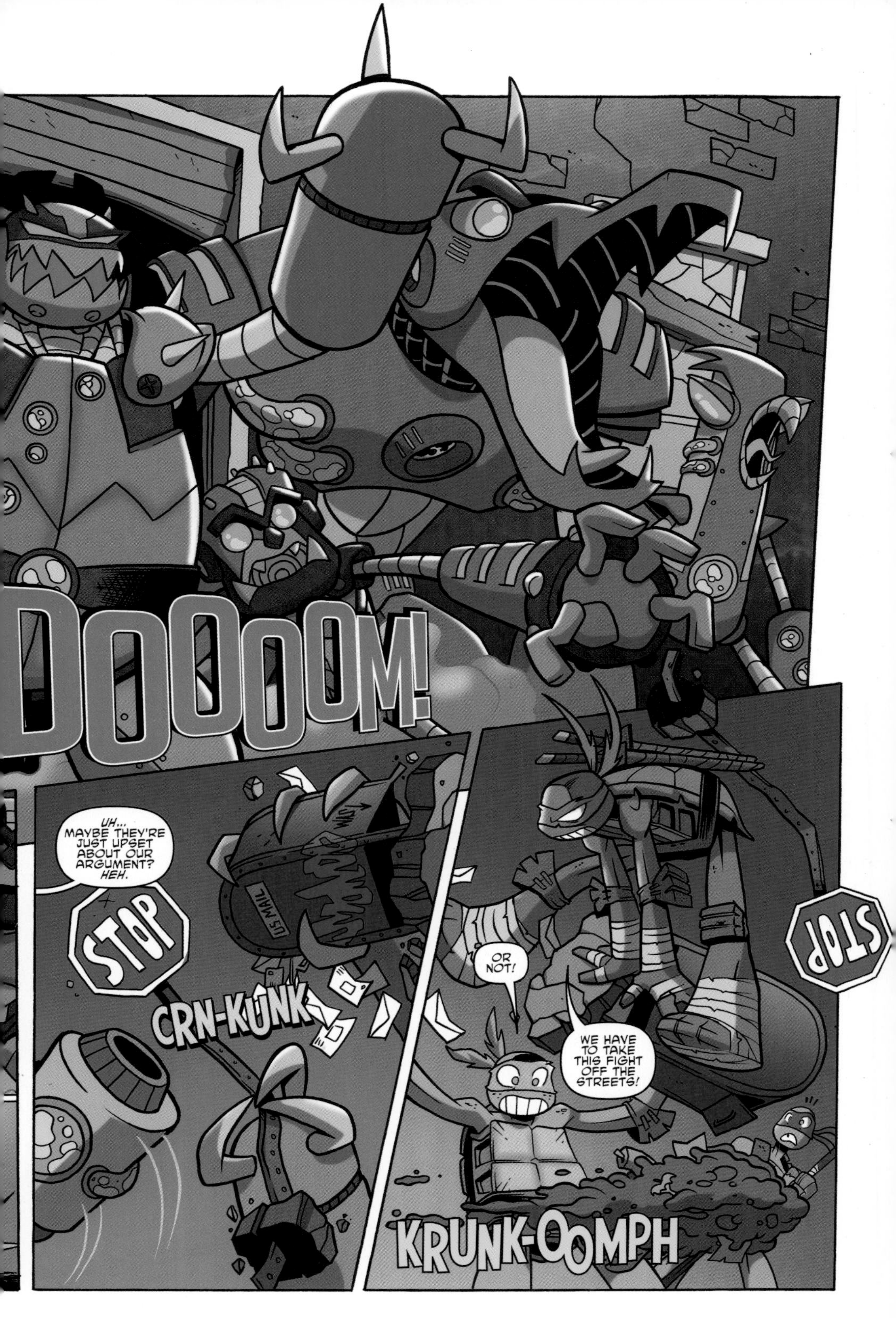
DOOOOOM!
UH... MAYBE THEY'RE JUST UPSET ABOUT OUR ARGUMENT? HEH.
STOP
US MAIL
CRN-KUNK
OR NOT!
WE HAVE TO TAKE THIS FIGHT OFF THE STREETS!
STOP
KRUNK-OOMPH

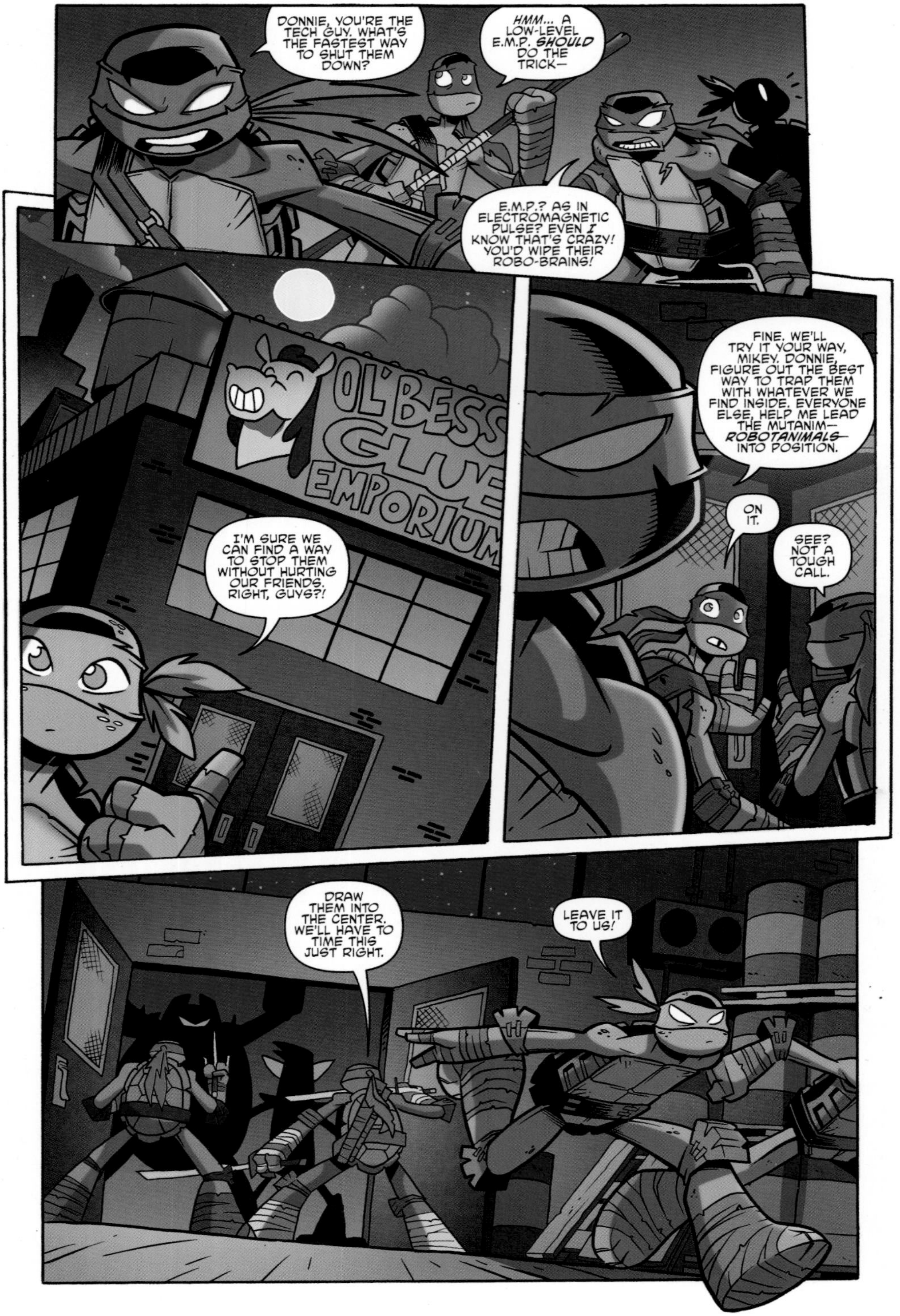
DONNIE, YOU'RE THE TECH GUY. WHAT'S THE FASTEST WAY TO SHUT THEM DOWN?
HMM... A LOW-LEVEL E.M.P. SHOULD DO THE TRICK—
E.M.P.? AS IN ELECTROMAGNETIC PULSE? EVEN I KNOW THAT'S CRAZY! YOU'D WIPE THEIR ROBO-BRAINS!
OL' BESS GLUE EMPORIUM
I'M SURE WE CAN FIND A WAY TO STOP THEM WITHOUT HURTING OUR FRIENDS. RIGHT, GUYS?!
FINE. WE'LL TRY IT YOUR WAY, MIKEY. DONNIE, FIGURE OUT THE BEST WAY TO TRAP THEM WITH WHATEVER WE FIND INSIDE. EVERYONE ELSE, HELP ME LEAD THE MUTANIM— ROBOTANIMALS— INTO POSITION.
ON IT.
SEE? NOT A TOUGH CALL.
DRAW THEM INTO THE CENTER. WE'LL HAVE TO TIME THIS JUST RIGHT.
LEAVE IT TO US!

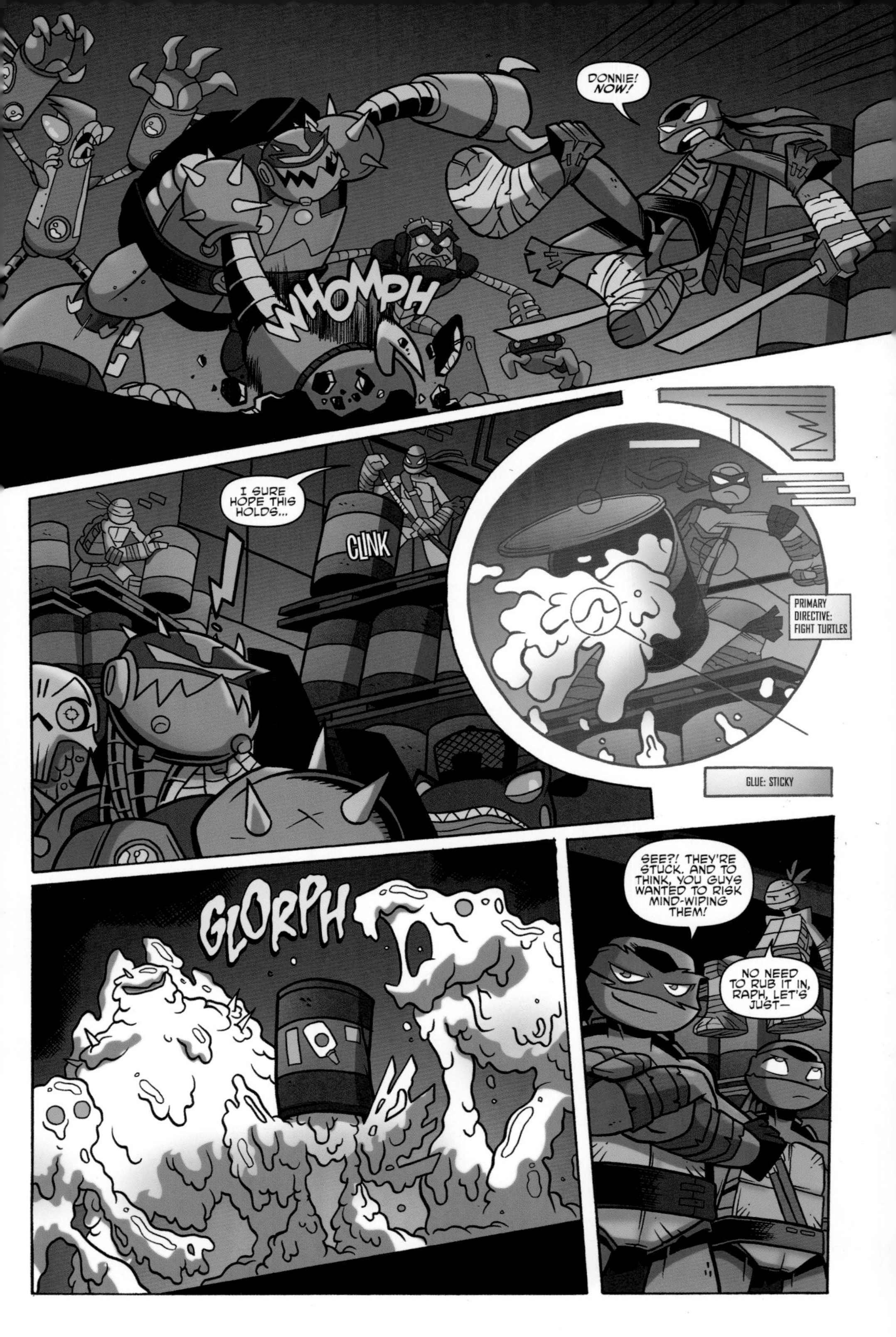
DONIE! NOW!
WHOMPH
I SURE HOPE THIS HOLDS...
CLINK
PRIMARY DIRECTIVE: FIGHT TURTLES
GLUE: STICKY
GLORPH
SEE?! THEY'RE STUCK. AND TO THINK, YOU GUYS WANTED TO RISK MIND-WIPING THEM!
NO NEED TO RUB IT IN, RAPH, LET'S JUST—

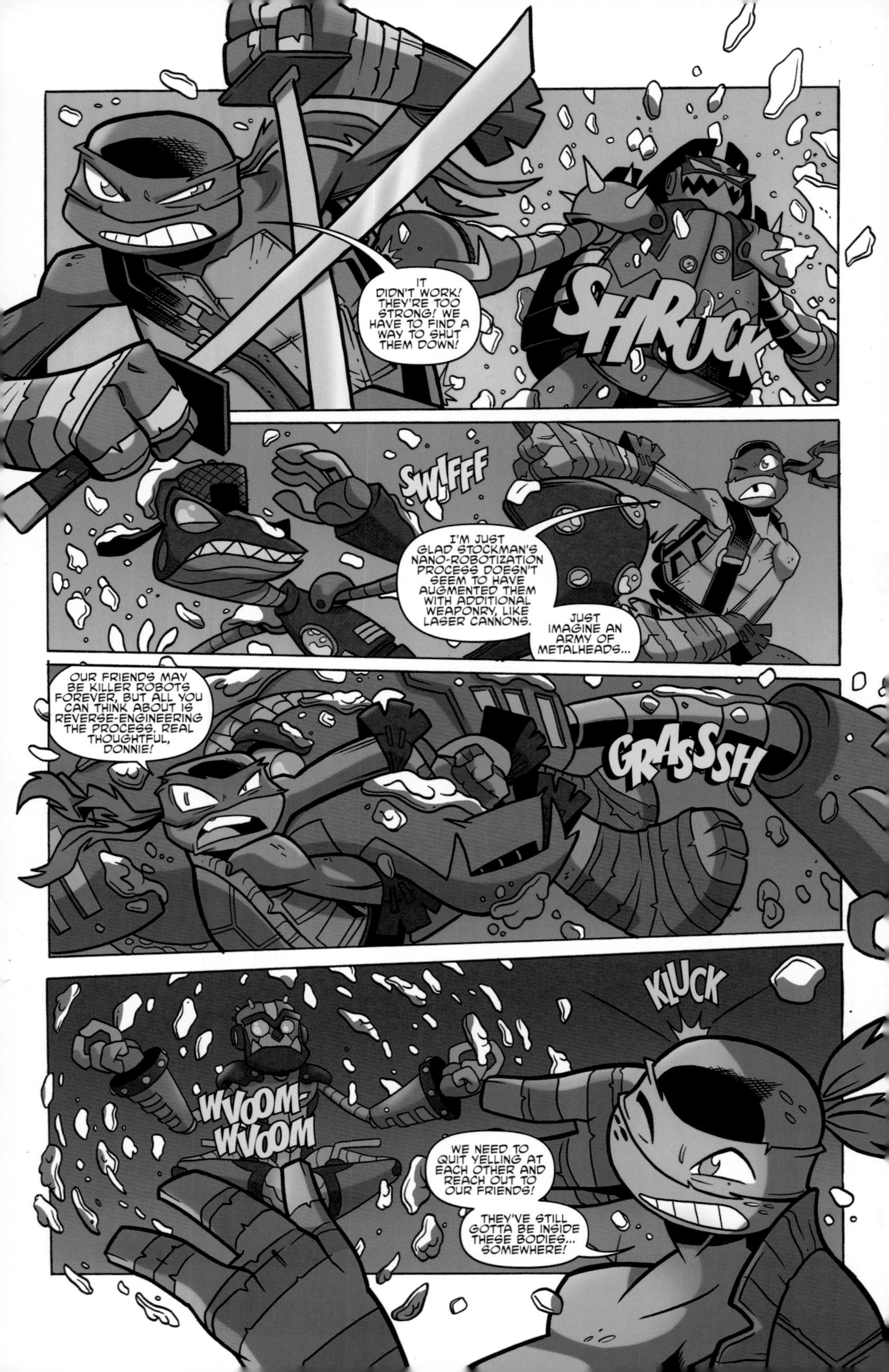
IT DIDN'T WORK! THEY'RE TOO STRONG! WE HAVE TO FIND A WAY TO SHUT THEM DOWN!
SHRUCK
SWIFFF
I'M JUST GLAD STOCKMAN'S NANO-ROBOTIZATION PROCESS DOESN'T SEEM TO HAVE AUGMENTED THEM WITH ADDITIONAL WEAPONRY, LIKE LASER CANNONS.
JUST IMAGINE AN ARMY OF METALHEADS...
OUR FRIENDS MAY BE KILLER ROBOTS FOREVER, BUT ALL YOU CAN THINK ABOUT IS REVERSE-ENGINEERING THE PROCESS. REAL THOUGHTFUL, DONNIE!
GRASSSH
KLUCK
WVOOM-WVOOM
WE NEED TO QUIT YELLING AT EACH OTHER AND REACH OUT TO OUR FRIENDS!
THEY'VE STILL GOTTA BE INSIDE THESE BODIES... SOMEWHERE!

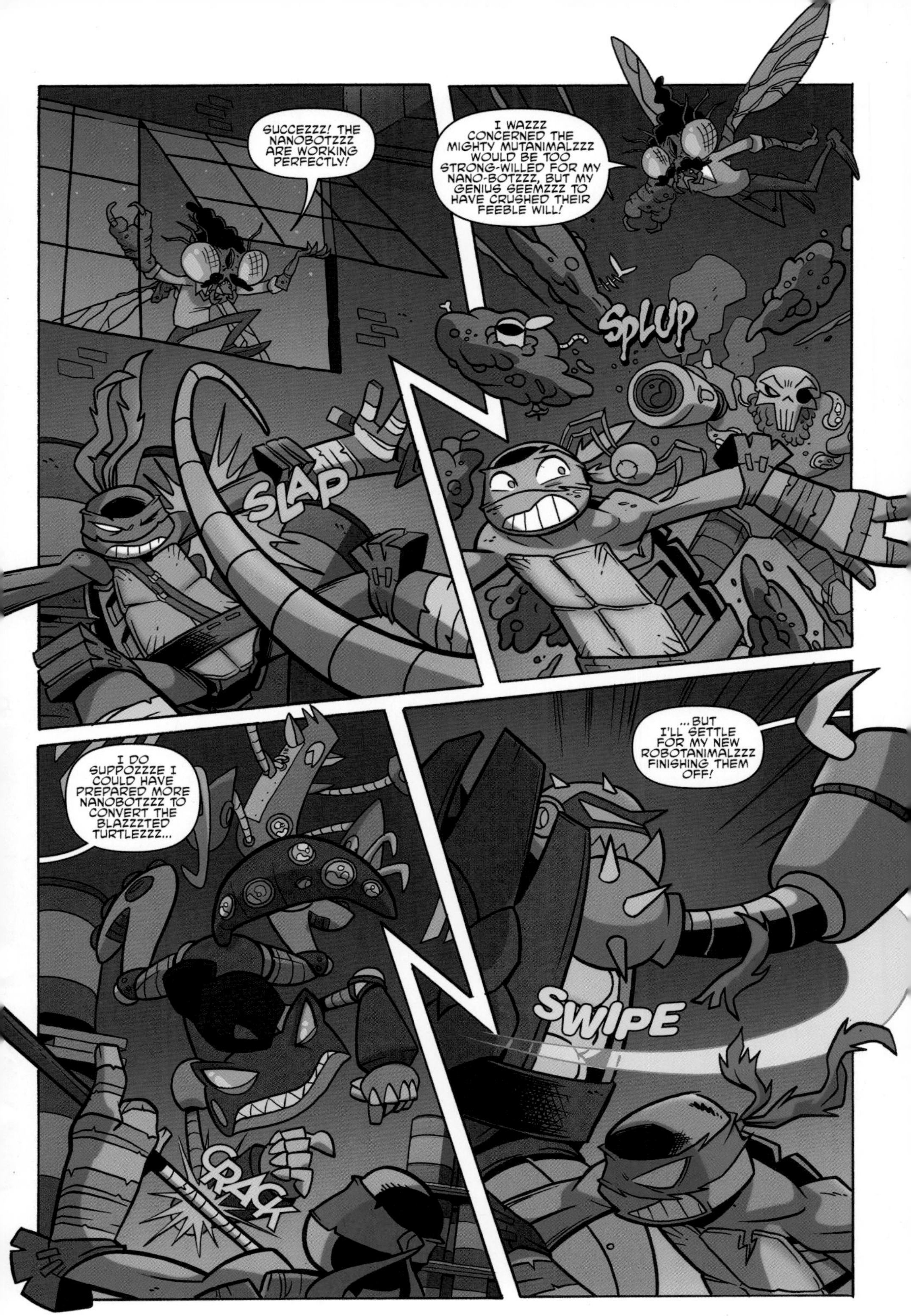
SUCCEZZZ! THE NANOBOTZZZ ARE WORKING PERFECTLY!
I WAZZZ CONCERNED THE MIGHTY MUTANIMALZZZ WOULD BE TOO STRONG-WILLED FOR MY NANO-BOTZZZ, BUT MY GENIUS SEEMZZZ TO HAVE CRUSHED THEIR FEEBLE WILL!
SPLUP
SLAP
I DO SUPPOZZZE I COULD HAVE PREPARED MORE NANOBOTZZZ TO CONVERT THE BLAZZZTED TURTLEZZZ...
CRACK
...BUT I'LL SETTLE FOR MY NEW ROBOTANIMALZZZ FINISHING THEM OFF!
SWIPE

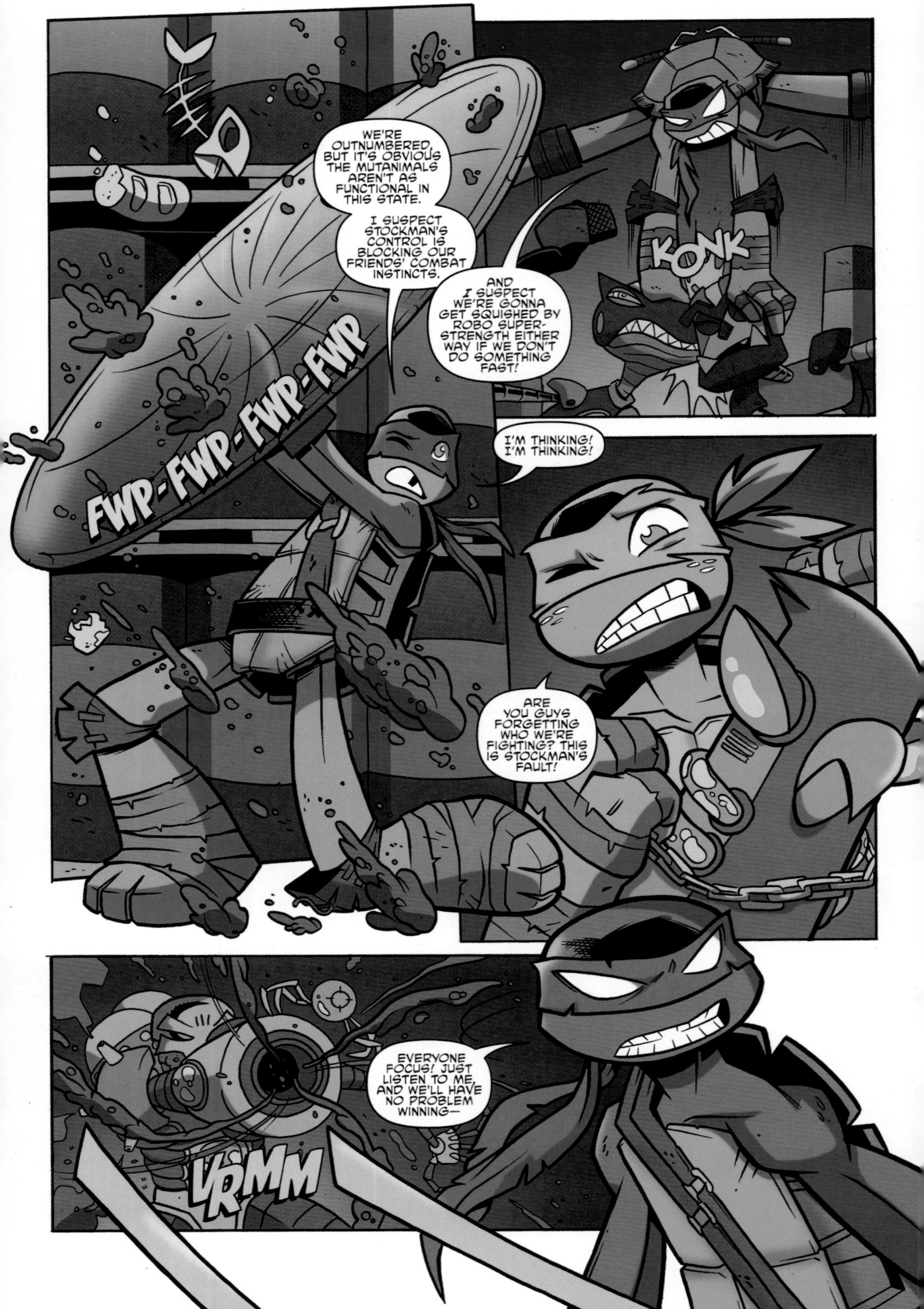
WE'RE OUTNUMBERED, BUT IT'S OBVIOUS THE MUTANIMALS AREN'T AS FUNCTIONAL IN THIS STATE.
I SUSPECT STOCKMAN'S CONTROL IS BLOCKING OUR FRIENDS' COMBAT INSTINCTS.
AND I SUSPECT WE'RE GONNA GET SQUISHED BY ROBO SUPER-STRENGTH EITHER WAY IF WE DON'T DO SOMETHING FAST!
KONK
FWP-FWP-FWP-FWP-FWP
I'M THINKING! I'M THINKING!
ARE YOU GUYS FORGETTING WHO WE'RE FIGHTING? THIS IS STOCKMAN'S FAULT!
EVERYONE FOCUS! JUST LISTEN TO ME, AND WE'LL HAVE NO PROBLEM WINNING—
VRMM

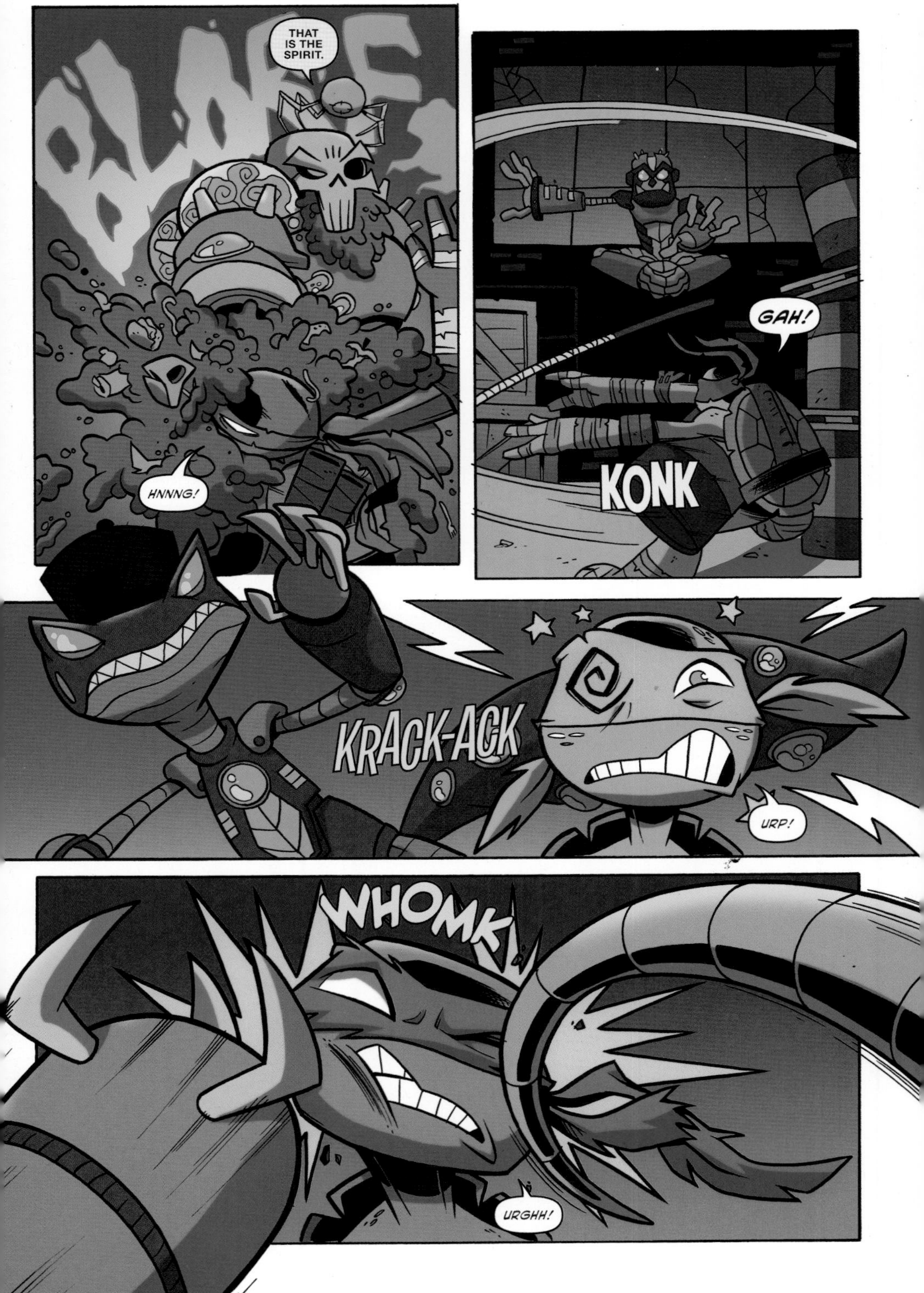
THAT IS THE SPIRIT.
BLAFF
HNNNG!
GAH!
KONK
KRACK-ACK
URP!
WHOMK
URGHH!

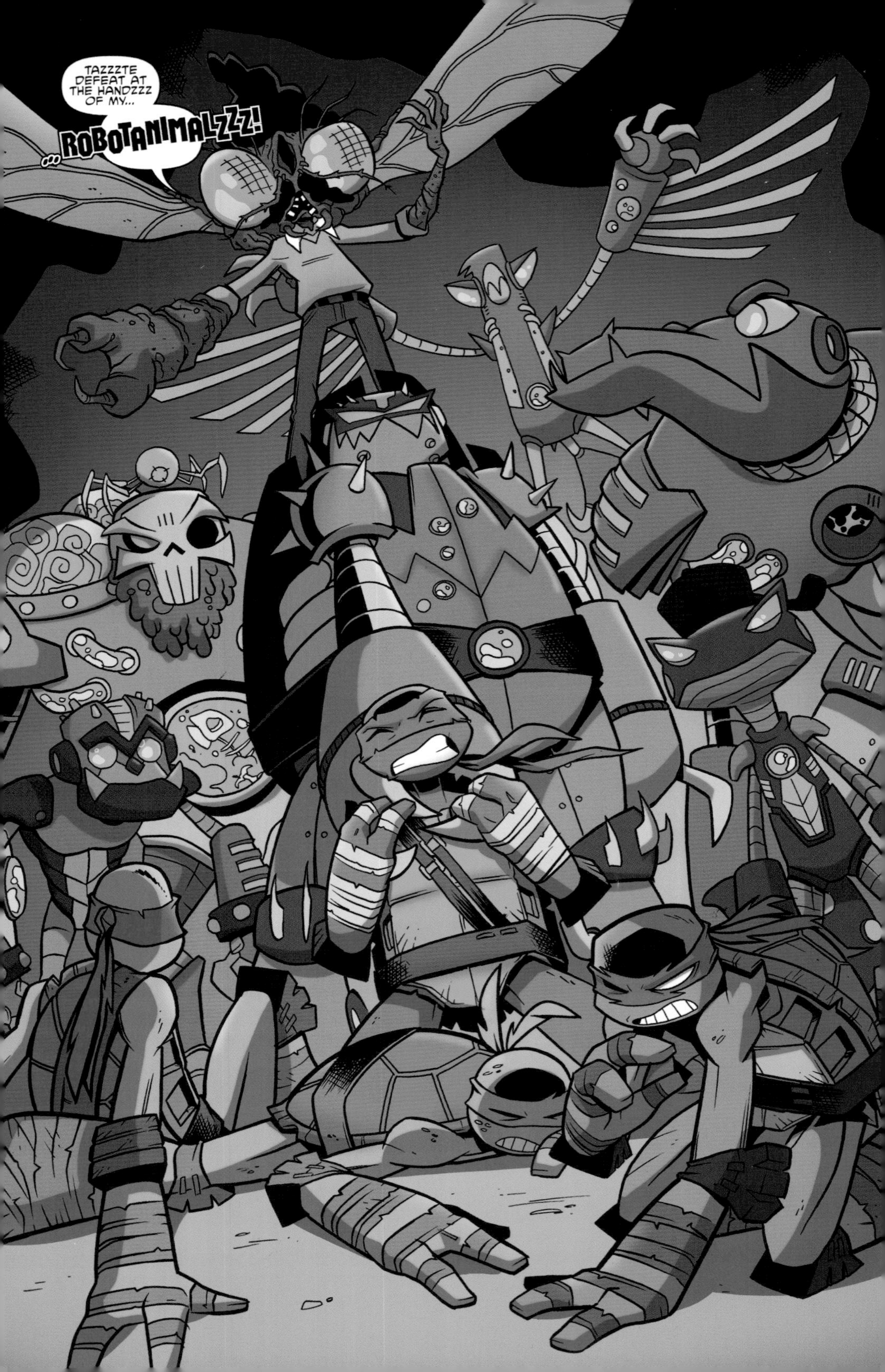
TAZZZTE DEFEAT AT THE HANDZZZ OF MY...
...ROBOTANIMALZZZ!

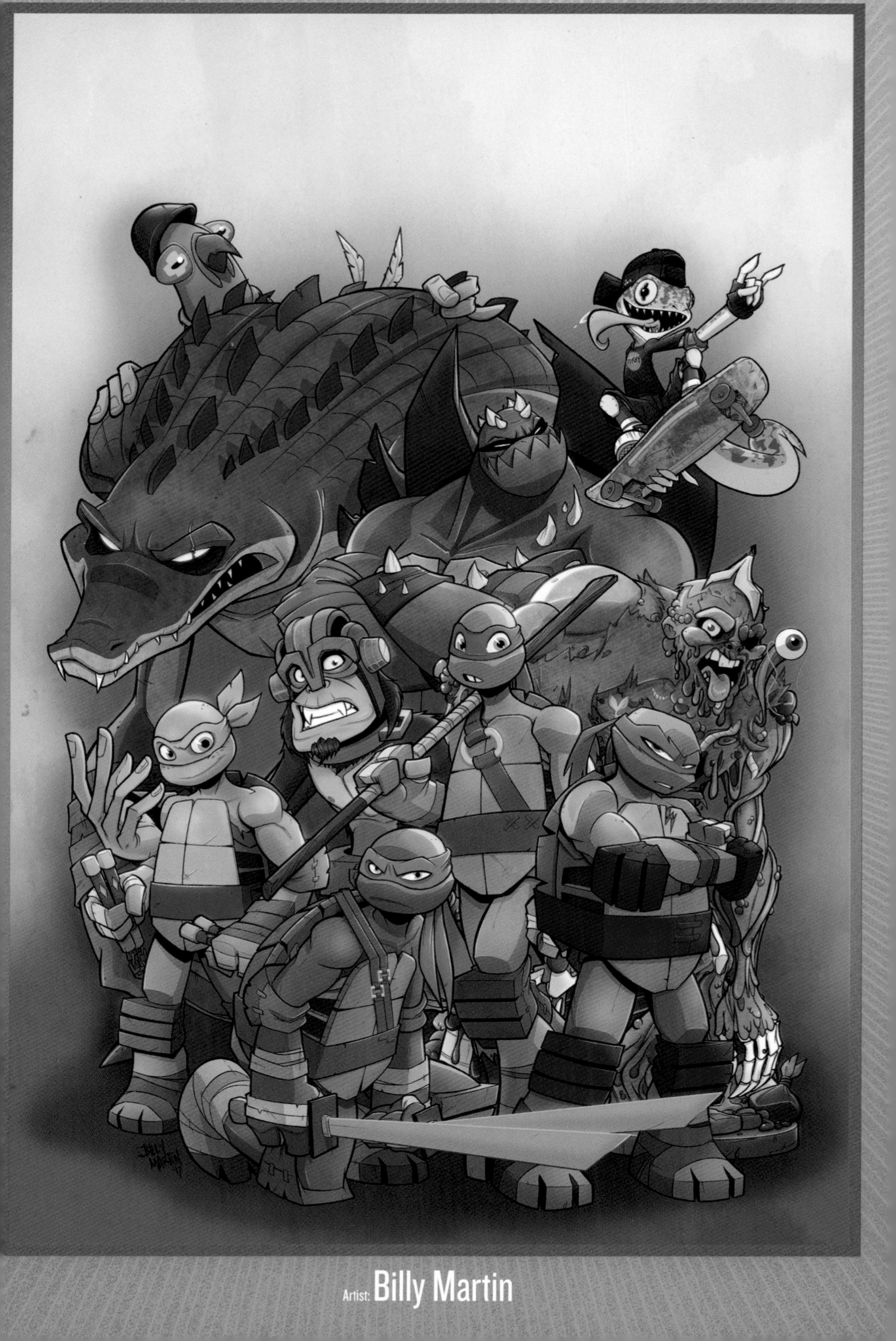

Artist: **Billy Martin**

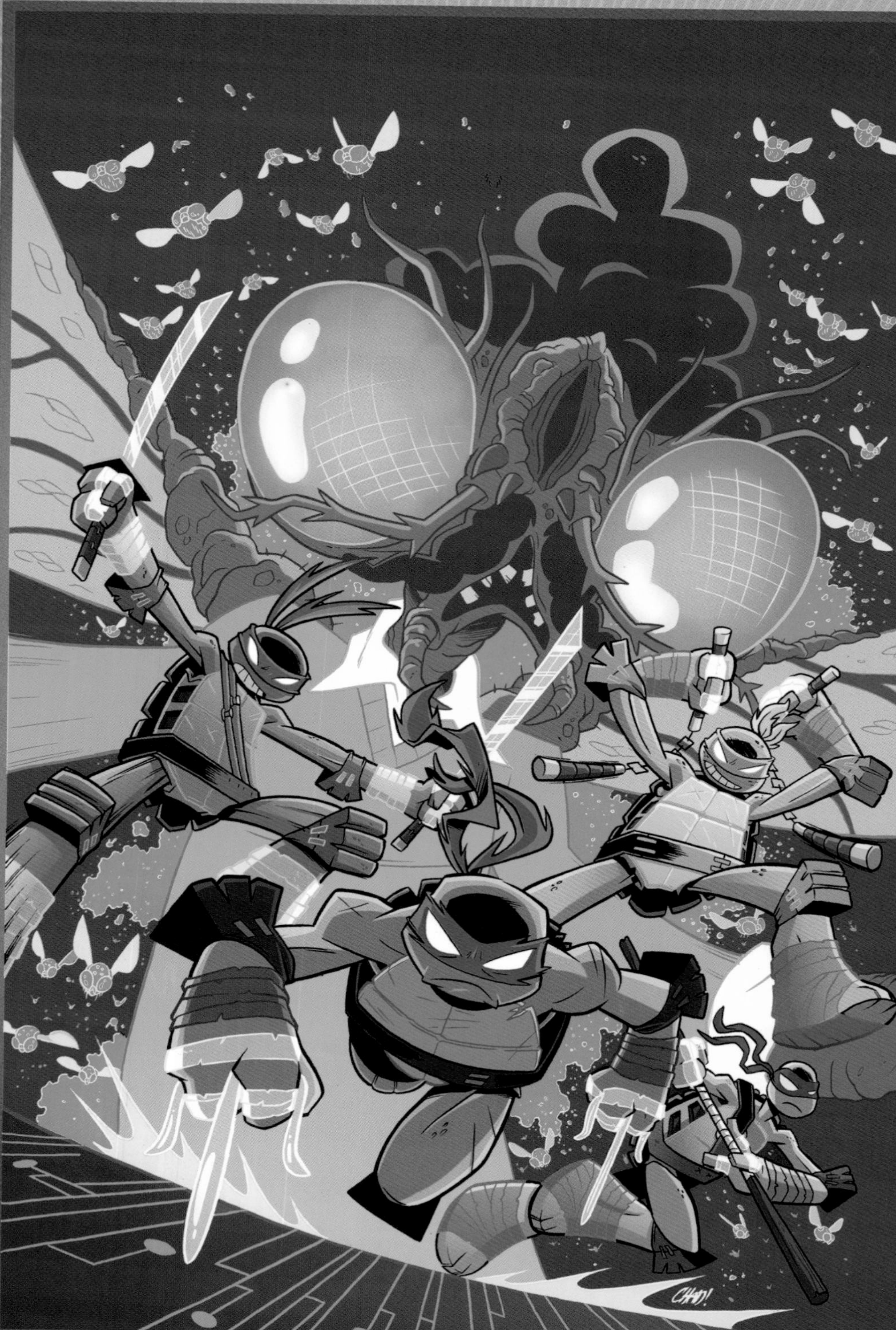

Artist: Chad Thomas

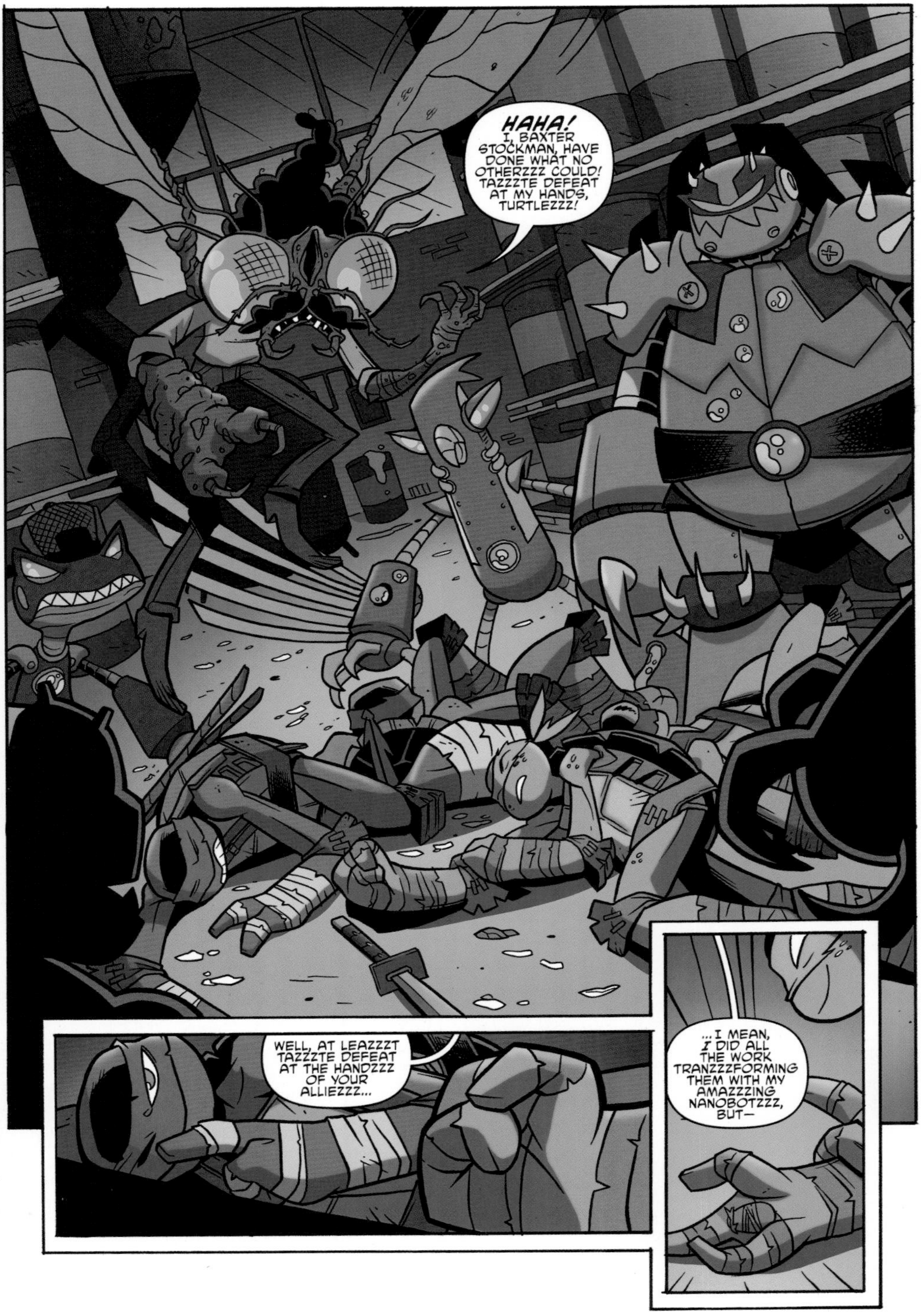
HAHA! I, BAXTER STOCKMAN, HAVE DONE WHAT NO OTHERZZZ COULD! TAZZZTE DEFEAT AT MY HANDS, TURTLEZZZ!
WELL, AT LEAZZZT TAZZZTE DEFEAT AT THE HANDZZZ OF YOUR ALLIEZZZ...
...I MEAN, I DID ALL THE WORK TRANZZZFORMING THEM WITH MY AMAZZZING NANOBOTZZZ, BUT—

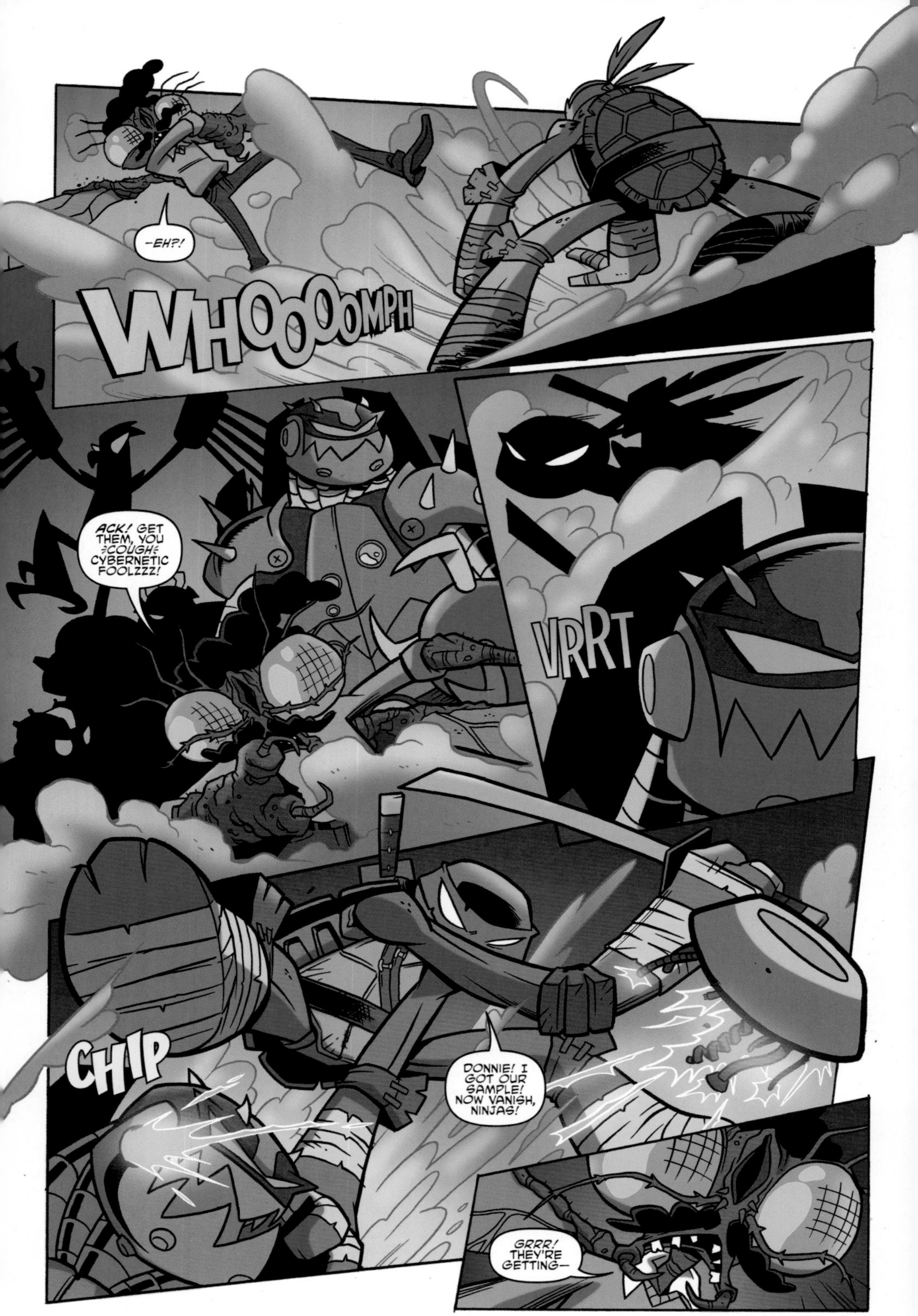

—EH?!
WHOOOOOMPH
ACK! GET THEM, YOU ≈COUGH≈ CYBERNETIC FOOLZZZ!
VRRT
CHIP
DONNIE! I GOT OUR SAMPLE! NOW VANISH, NINJAS!
GRRR! THEY'RE GETTING—

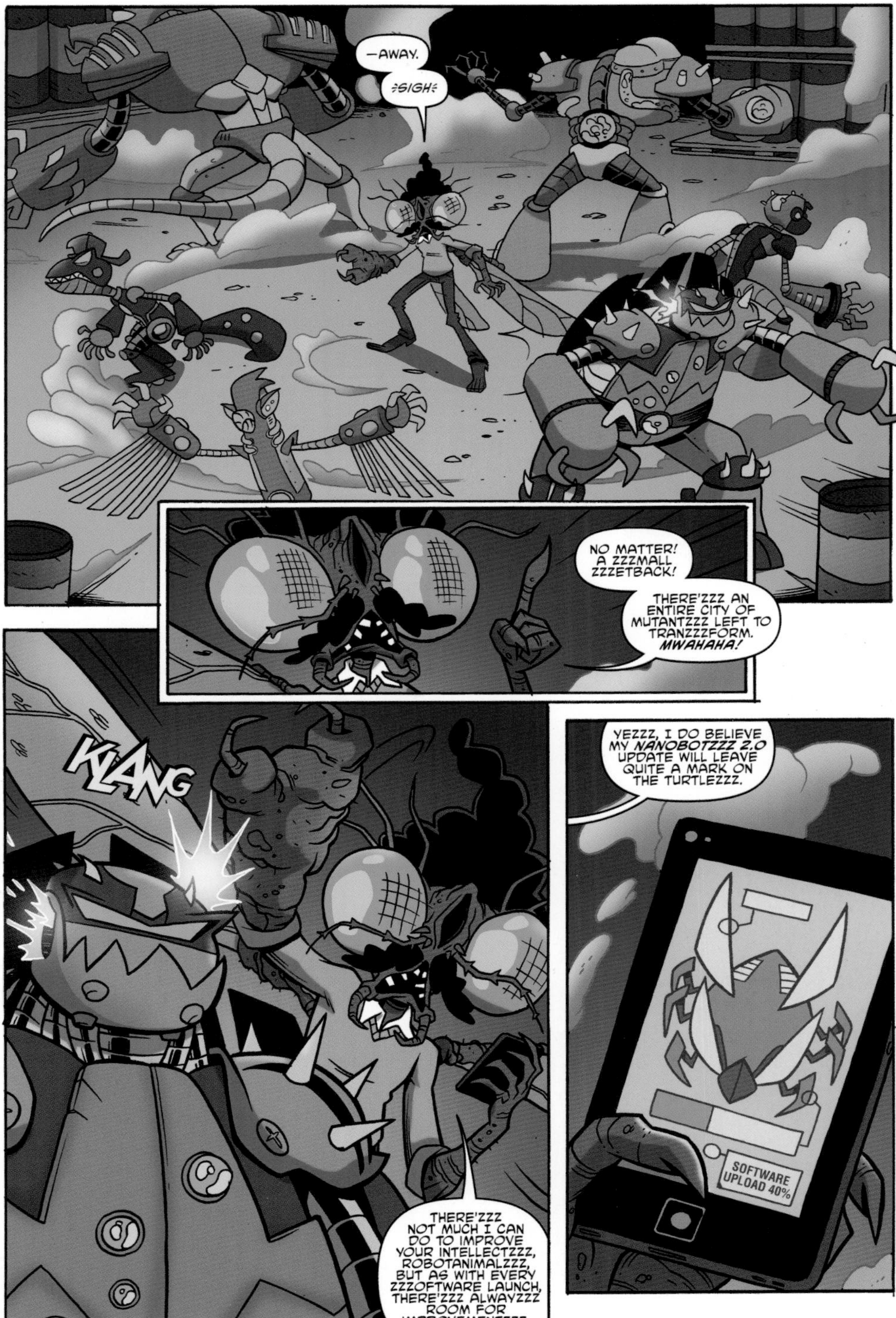

—AWAY.
SIGH
NO MATTER! A ZZZMALL ZZZETBACK!
THERE'ZZZ AN ENTIRE CITY OF MUTANTZZZ LEFT TO TRANZZZFORM. MWAHAHA!
KLANG
THERE'ZZZ NOT MUCH I CAN DO TO IMPROVE YOUR INTELLECTZZZ, ROBOTANIMALZZZ, BUT AS WITH EVERY ZZZOFTWARE LAUNCH, THERE'ZZZ ALWAYZZZ ROOM FOR IMPROVEMENTZZZ.
YEZZZ, I DO BELIEVE MY NANOBOTZZZ 2.0 UPDATE WILL LEAVE QUITE A MARK ON THE TURTLEZZZ.
SOFTWARE UPLOAD 40%

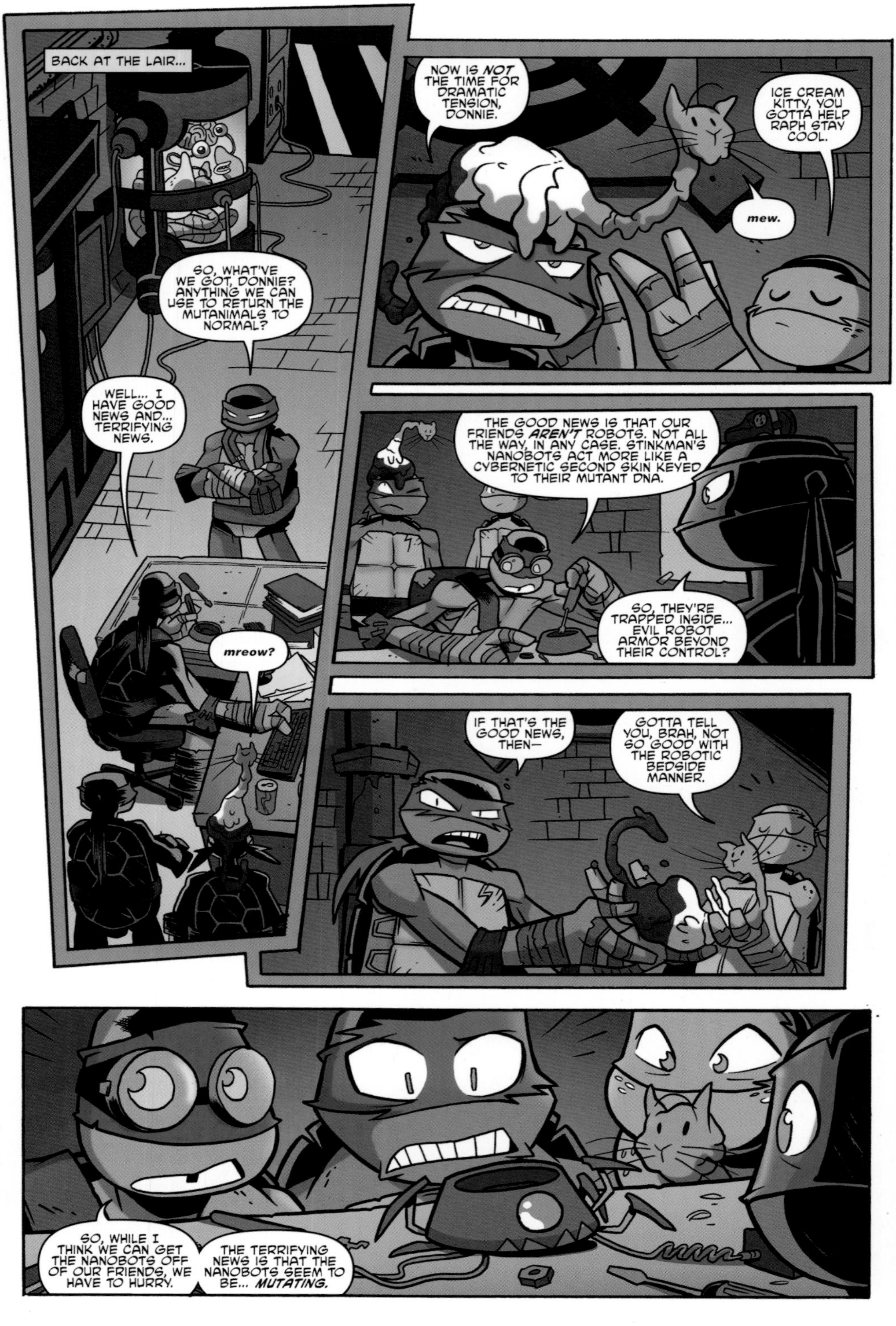
BACK AT THE LAIR...
SO, WHAT'VE WE GOT, DONNIE? ANYTHING WE CAN USE TO RETURN THE MUTANIMALS TO NORMAL?
WELL... I HAVE GOOD NEWS AND... TERRIFYING NEWS.
mreow?
NOW IS NOT THE TIME FOR DRAMATIC TENSION, DONNIE.
ICE CREAM KITTY, YOU GOTTA HELP RAPH STAY COOL.
mew.
THE GOOD NEWS IS THAT OUR FRIENDS AREN'T ROBOTS. NOT ALL THE WAY, IN ANY CASE. STINKMAN'S NANOBOTS ACT MORE LIKE A CYBERNETIC SECOND SKIN KEYED TO THEIR MUTANT DNA.
SO, THEY'RE TRAPPED INSIDE... EVIL ROBOT ARMOR BEYOND THEIR CONTROL?
IF THAT'S THE GOOD NEWS, THEN—
GOTTA TELL YOU, BRAH, NOT SO GOOD WITH THE ROBOTIC BEDSIDE MANNER.
SO, WHILE I THINK WE CAN GET THE NANOBOTS OFF OF OUR FRIENDS, WE HAVE TO HURRY.
THE TERRIFYING NEWS IS THAT THE NANOBOTS SEEM TO BE... MUTATING.

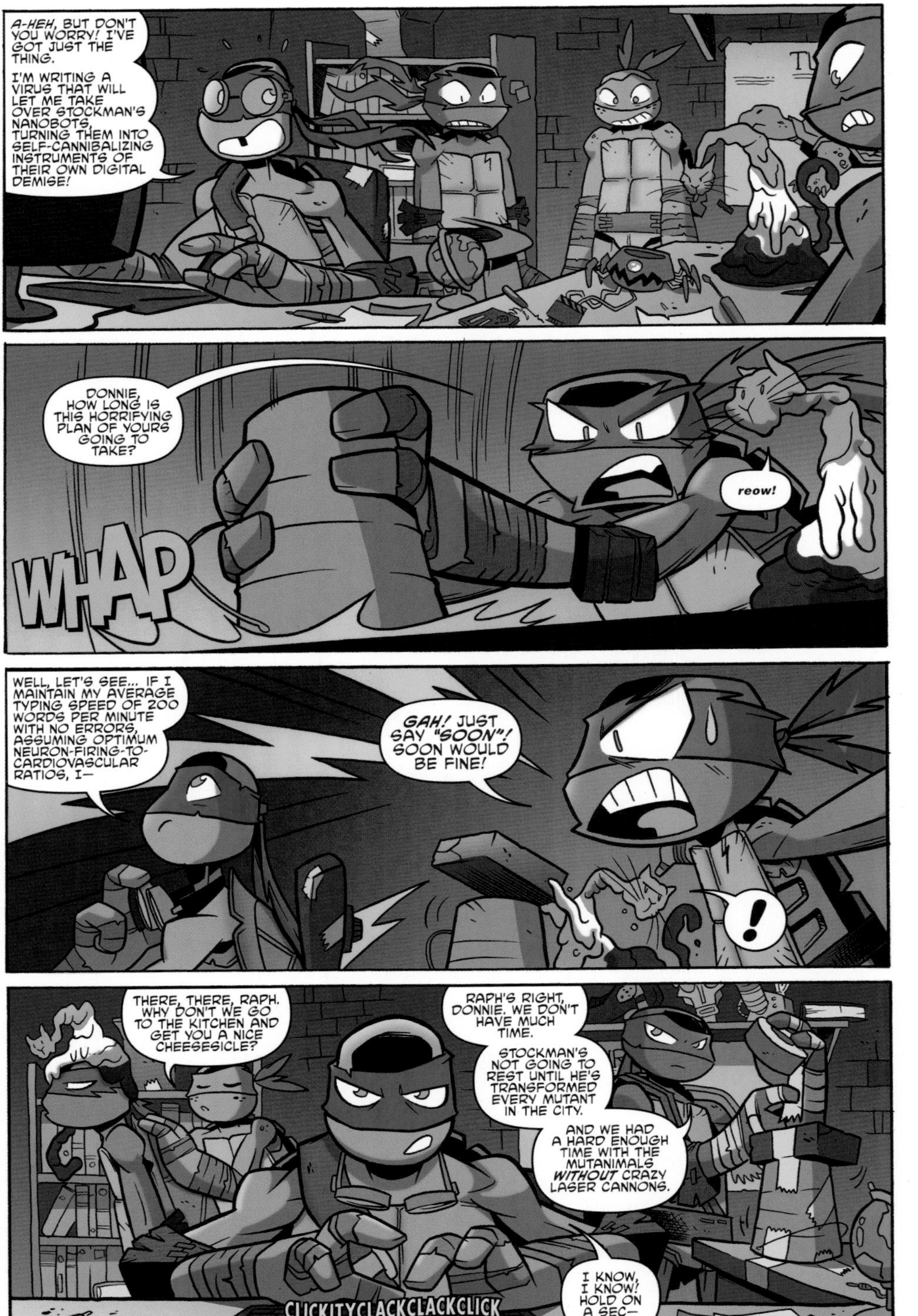
A-HEH, BUT DON'T YOU WORRY! I'VE GOT JUST THE THING.
I'M WRITING A VIRUS THAT WILL LET ME TAKE OVER STOCKMAN'S NANOBOTS, TURNING THEM INTO SELF-CANNIBALIZING INSTRUMENTS OF THEIR OWN DIGITAL DEMISE!
DONNIE, HOW LONG IS THIS HORRIFYING PLAN OF YOURS GOING TO TAKE?
reow!
WHAP
WELL, LET'S SEE... IF I MAINTAIN MY AVERAGE TYPING SPEED OF 200 WORDS PER MINUTE WITH NO ERRORS, ASSUMING OPTIMUM NEURON-FIRING-TO-CARDIOVASCULAR RATIOS, I—
GAH! JUST SAY "SOON"! SOON WOULD BE FINE!
!
THERE, THERE, RAPH. WHY DON'T WE GO TO THE KITCHEN AND GET YOU A NICE CHEESESICLE?
RAPH'S RIGHT, DONNIE. WE DON'T HAVE MUCH TIME.
STOCKMAN'S NOT GOING TO REST UNTIL HE'S TRANSFORMED EVERY MUTANT IN THE CITY.
AND WE HAD A HARD ENOUGH TIME WITH THE MUTANIMALS WITHOUT CRAZY LASER CANNONS.
I KNOW, I KNOW! HOLD ON A SEC—
CLICKITYCLACKCLACKCLICK

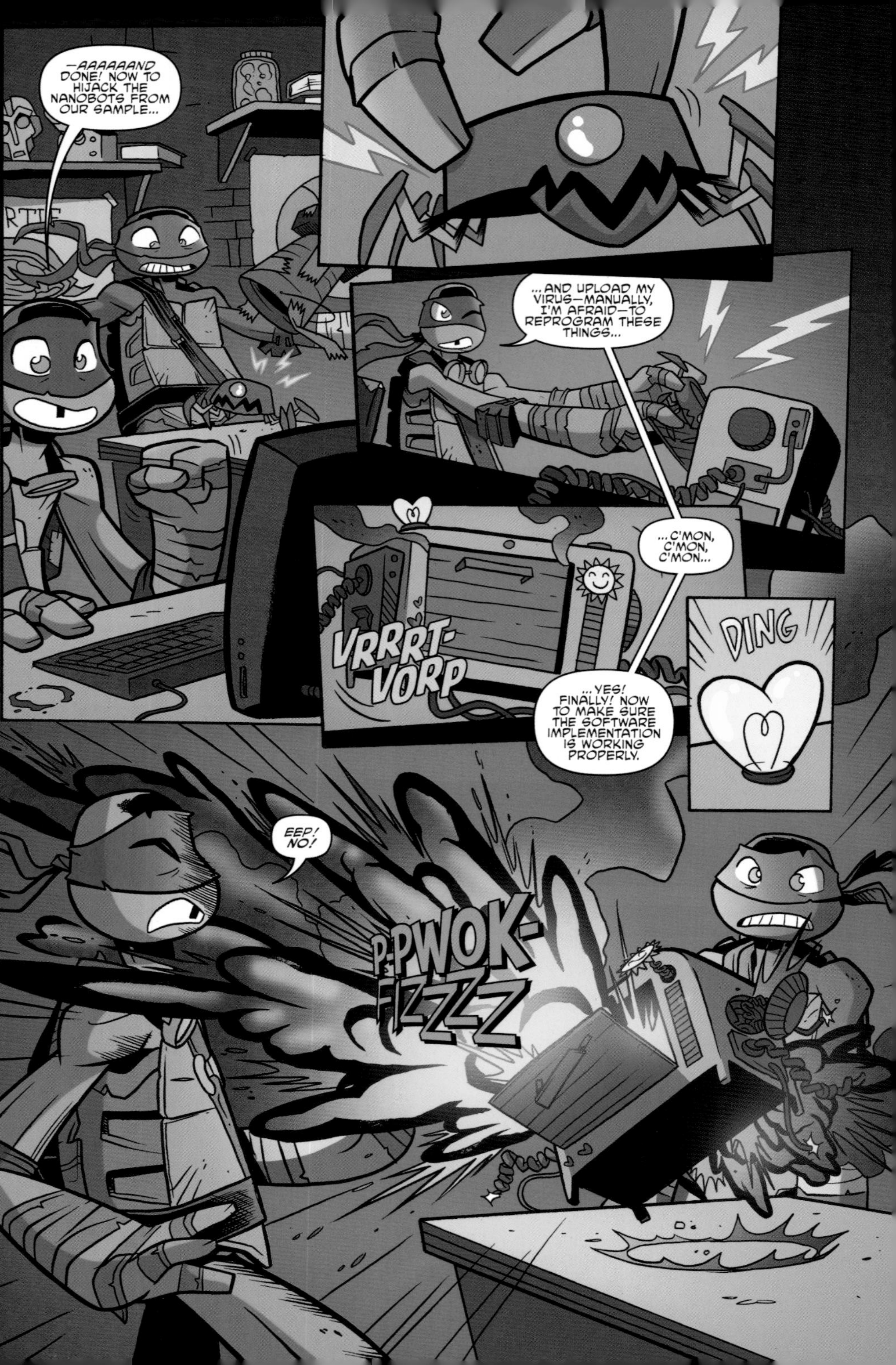
—AAAAAAND DONE! NOW TO HIJACK THE NANOBOTS FROM OUR SAMPLE...
...AND UPLOAD MY VIRUS—MANUALLY, I'M AFRAID—TO REPROGRAM THESE THINGS...
...C'MON, C'MON, C'MON...
VRRRT-VORP
DING
...YES! FINALLY! NOW TO MAKE SURE THE SOFTWARE IMPLEMENTATION IS WORKING PROPERLY.
EEP! NO!
P-PWOK-FIZZZZ

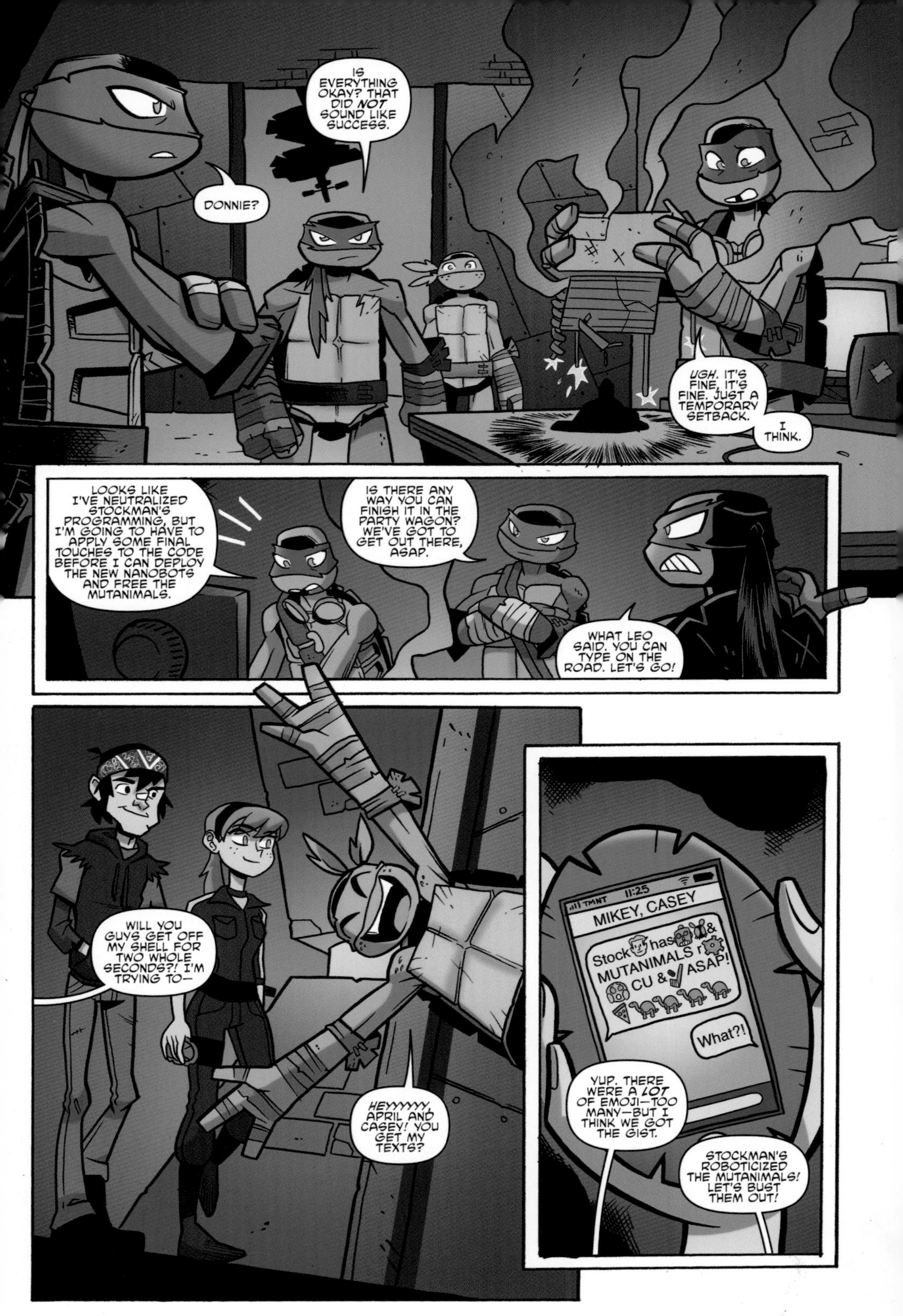
IS EVERYTHING OKAY? THAT DID *NOT* SOUND LIKE SUCCESS.
DONNIE?
UGH. IT'S FINE, IT'S FINE. JUST A TEMPORARY SETBACK.
I THINK.
LOOKS LIKE I'VE NEUTRALIZED STOCKMAN'S PROGRAMMING, BUT I'M GOING TO HAVE TO APPLY SOME FINAL TOUCHES TO THE CODE BEFORE I CAN DEPLOY THE NEW NANOBOTS AND FREE THE MUTANIMALS.
IS THERE ANY WAY YOU CAN FINISH IT IN THE PARTY WAGON? WE'VE GOT TO GET OUT THERE, ASAP.
WHAT LEO SAID. YOU CAN TYPE ON THE ROAD. LET'S GO!
WILL YOU GUYS GET OFF MY SHELL FOR TWO WHOLE SECONDS?! I'M TRYING TO—
HEYYYYYY, APRIL AND CASEY! YOU GET MY TEXTS?
TMNT
11:25
MIKEY, CASEY
Stock has &
MUTANIMALS r
CU & ASAP!
What?!
YUP. THERE WERE A *LOT* OF EMOJI—TOO MANY—BUT I THINK WE GOT THE GIST.
STOCKMAN'S ROBOTICIZED THE MUTANIMALS! LET'S BUST THEM OUT!

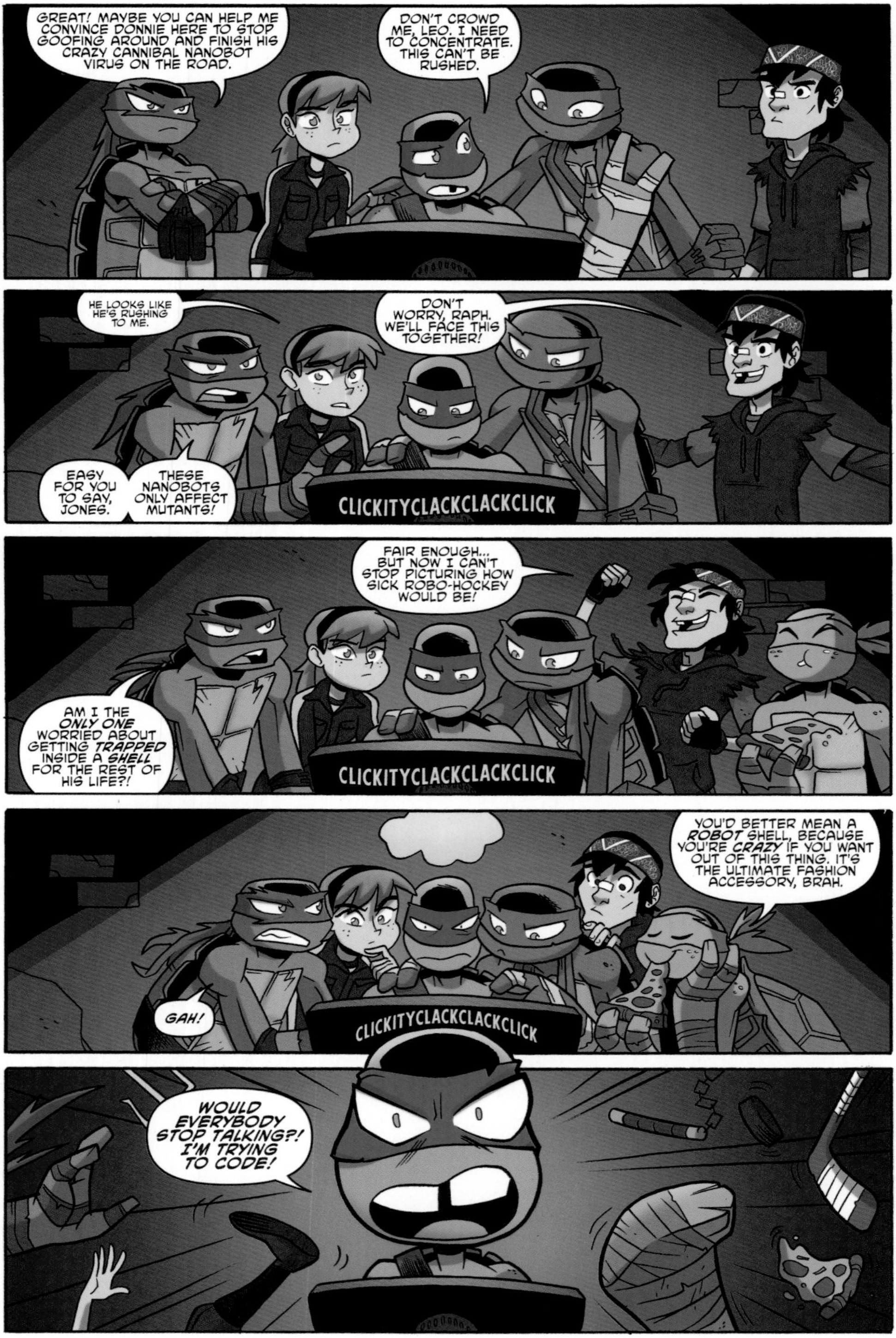
GREAT! MAYBE YOU CAN HELP ME CONVINCE DONNIE HERE TO STOP GOOFING AROUND AND FINISH HIS CRAZY CANNIBAL NANOBOT VIRUS ON THE ROAD.
DON'T CROWD ME, LEO. I NEED TO CONCENTRATE. THIS CAN'T BE RUSHED.
HE LOOKS LIKE HE'S RUSHING TO ME.
DON'T WORRY, RAPH. WE'LL FACE THIS TOGETHER!
EASY FOR YOU TO SAY, JONES.
THESE NANOBOTS ONLY AFFECT MUTANTS!
CLICKITYCLACKCLACKCLICK
FAIR ENOUGH... BUT NOW I CAN'T STOP PICTURING HOW SICK ROBO-HOCKEY WOULD BE!
AM I THE ONLY ONE WORRIED ABOUT GETTING TRAPPED INSIDE A SHELL FOR THE REST OF HIS LIFE?!
CLICKITYCLACKCLACKCLICK
YOU'D BETTER MEAN A ROBOT SHELL, BECAUSE YOU'RE CRAZY IF YOU WANT OUT OF THIS THING. IT'S THE ULTIMATE FASHION ACCESSORY, BRAH.
GAH!
CLICKITYCLACKCLACKCLICK
WOULD EVERYBODY STOP TALKING?! I'M TRYING TO CODE!

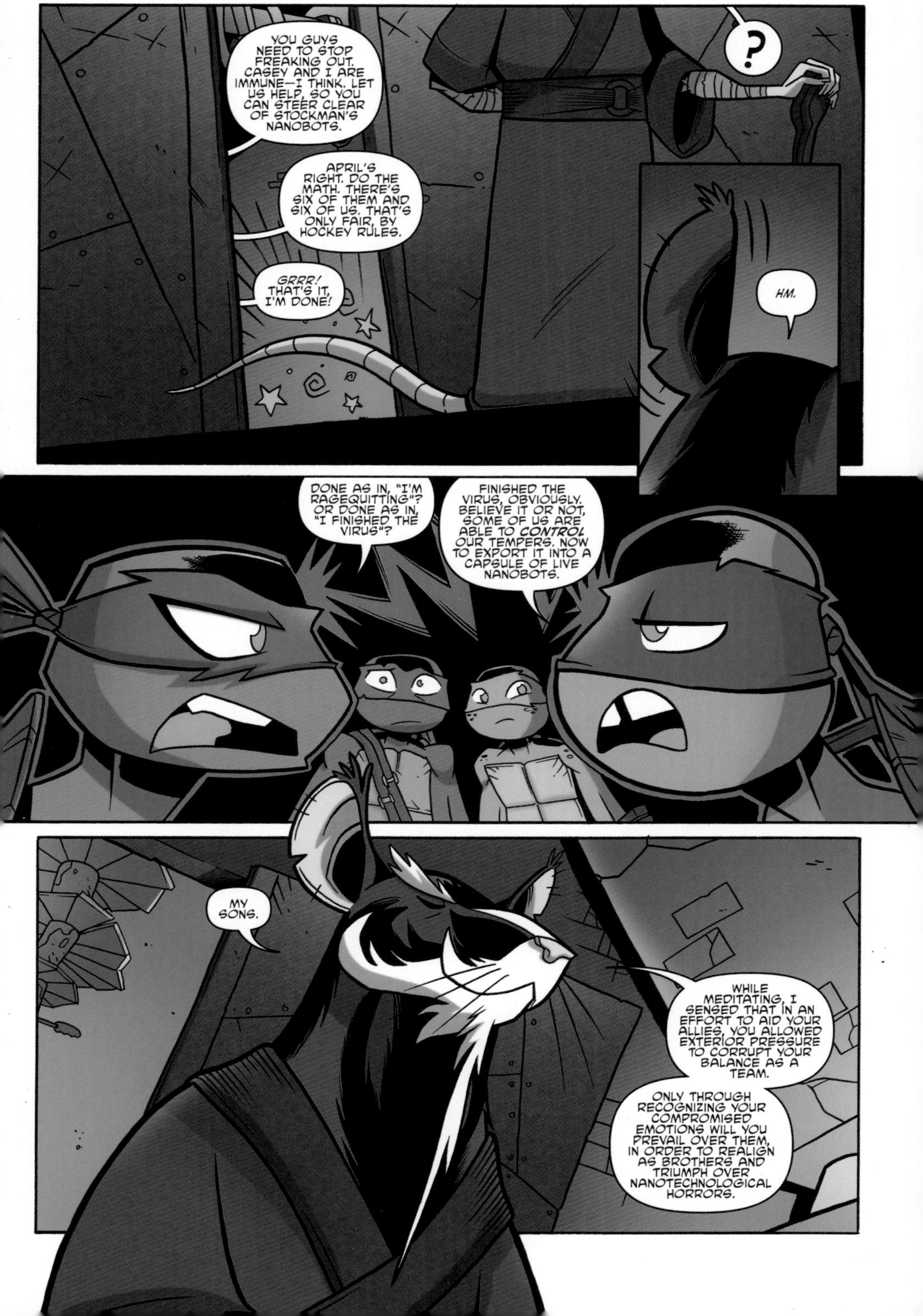
YOU GUYS NEED TO STOP FREAKING OUT. CASEY AND I ARE IMMUNE—I THINK. LET US HELP, SO YOU CAN STEER CLEAR OF STOCKMAN'S NANOBOTS.
?
APRIL'S RIGHT. DO THE MATH. THERE'S SIX OF THEM AND SIX OF US. THAT'S ONLY FAIR, BY HOCKEY RULES.
GRRR! THAT'S IT, I'M DONE!
HM.
DONE AS IN, "I'M RAGEQUITTING"? OR DONE AS IN, "I FINISHED THE VIRUS"?
FINISHED THE VIRUS, OBVIOUSLY. BELIEVE IT OR NOT, SOME OF US ARE ABLE TO CONTROL OUR TEMPERS. NOW TO EXPORT IT INTO A CAPSULE OF LIVE NANOBOTS.
MY SONS.
WHILE MEDITATING, I SENSED THAT IN AN EFFORT TO AID YOUR ALLIES, YOU ALLOWED EXTERIOR PRESSURE TO CORRUPT YOUR BALANCE AS A TEAM.
ONLY THROUGH RECOGNIZING YOUR COMPROMISED EMOTIONS WILL YOU PREVAIL OVER THEM, IN ORDER TO REALIGN AS BROTHERS AND TRIUMPH OVER NANOTECHNOLOGICAL HORRORS.

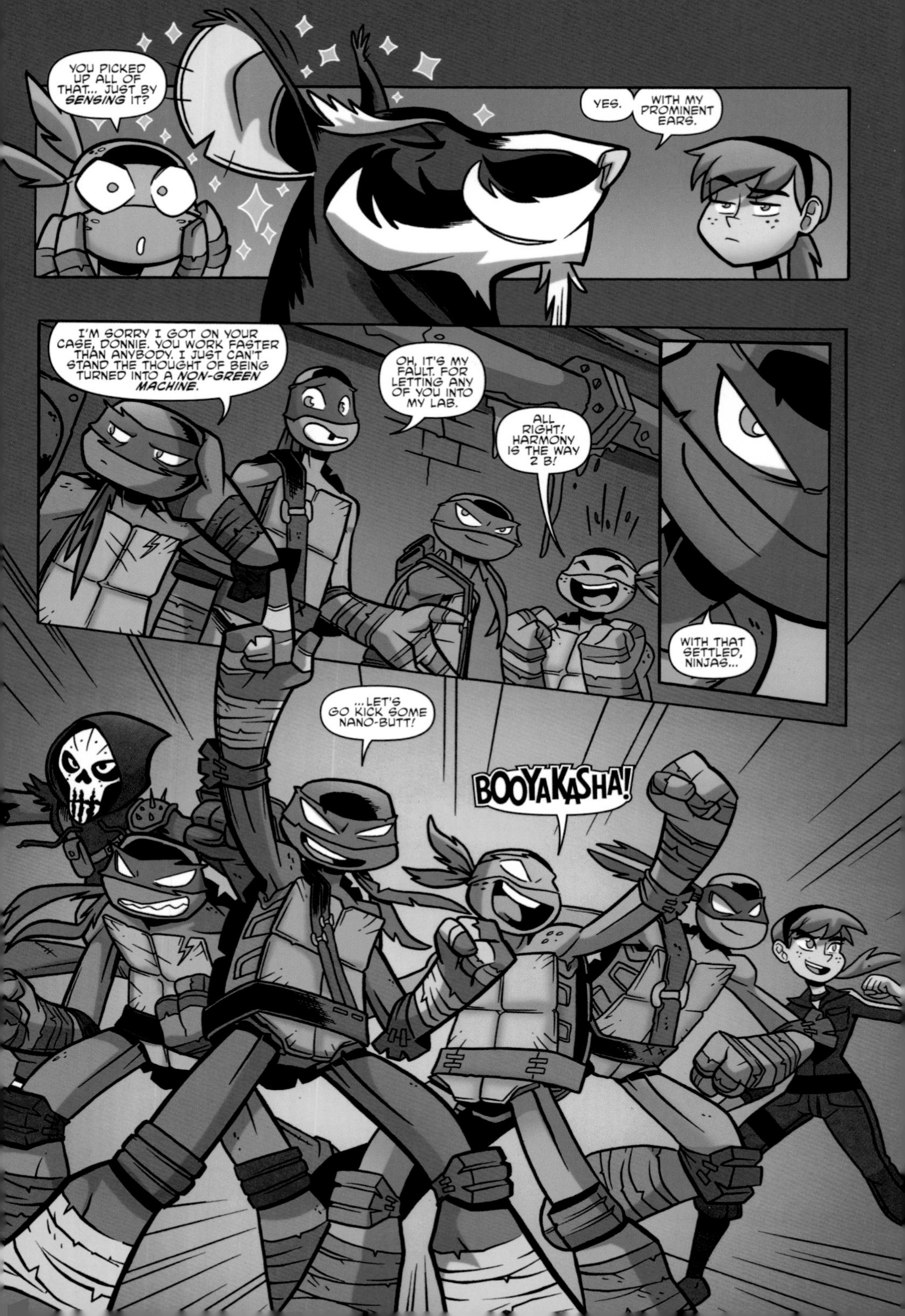
YOU PICKED UP ALL OF THAT... JUST BY *SENSING* IT?
YES.
WITH MY PROMINENT EARS.
I'M SORRY I GOT ON YOUR CASE, DONNIE. YOU WORK FASTER THAN ANYBODY. I JUST CAN'T STAND THE THOUGHT OF BEING TURNED INTO A *NON-GREEN MACHINE*.
OH, IT'S MY FAULT. FOR LETTING ANY OF YOU INTO MY LAB.
ALL RIGHT! HARMONY IS THE WAY 2 B!
WITH THAT SETTLED, NINJAS...
...LET'S GO KICK SOME NANO-BUTT!
BOOYAKASHA!

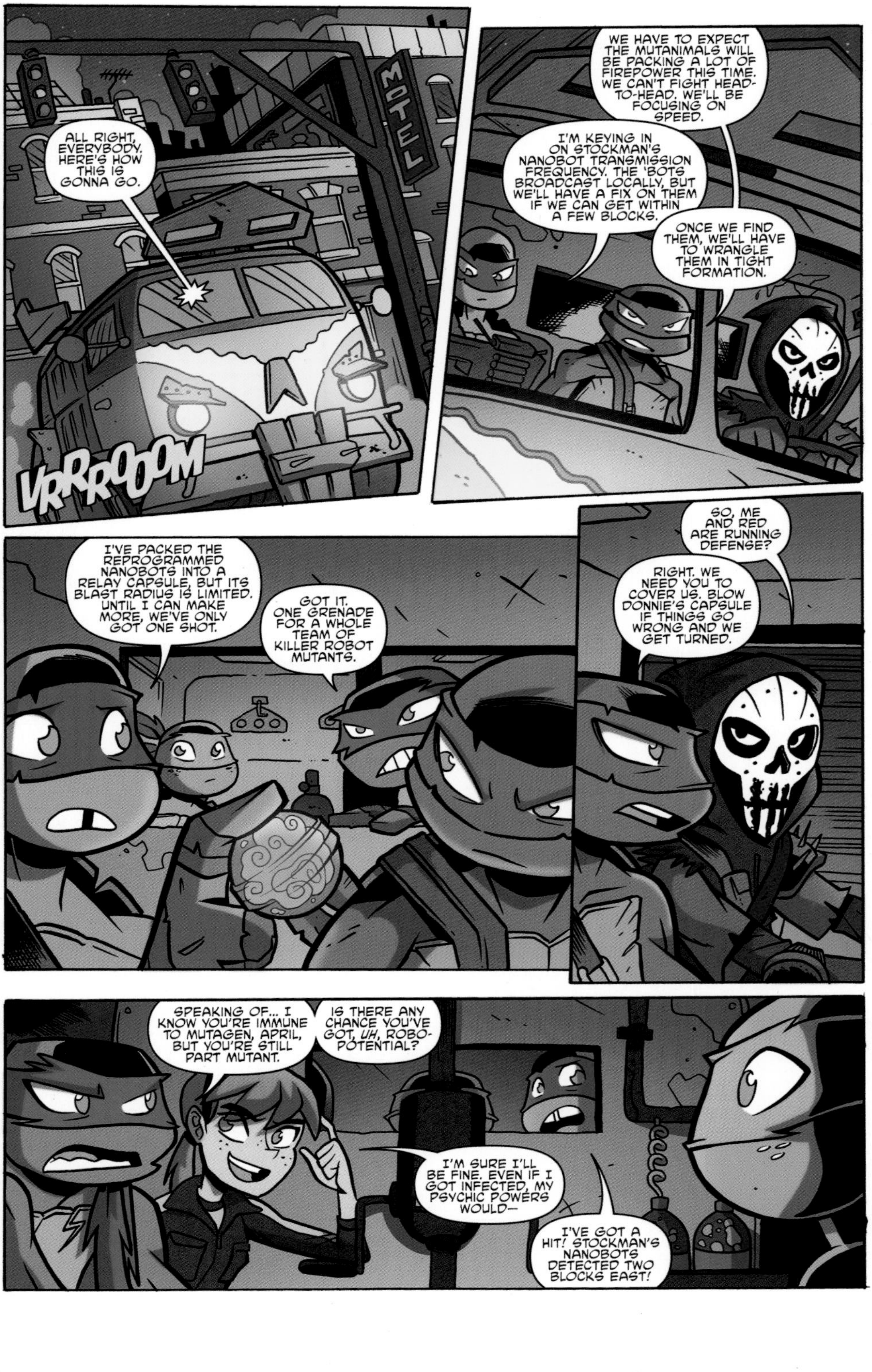
MOTEL
ALL RIGHT, EVERYBODY. HERE'S HOW THIS IS GONNA GO.
VRRROOOM
WE HAVE TO EXPECT THE MUTANIMALS WILL BE PACKING A LOT OF FIREPOWER THIS TIME. WE CAN'T FIGHT HEAD-TO-HEAD. WE'LL BE FOCUSING ON SPEED.
I'M KEYING IN ON STOCKMAN'S NANOBOT TRANSMISSION FREQUENCY. THE 'BOTS BROADCAST LOCALLY, BUT WE'LL HAVE A FIX ON THEM IF WE CAN GET WITHIN A FEW BLOCKS.
ONCE WE FIND THEM, WE'LL HAVE TO WRANGLE THEM IN TIGHT FORMATION.
I'VE PACKED THE REPROGRAMMED NANOBOTS INTO A RELAY CAPSULE, BUT ITS BLAST RADIUS IS LIMITED. UNTIL I CAN MAKE MORE, WE'VE ONLY GOT ONE SHOT.
GOT IT. ONE GRENADE FOR A WHOLE TEAM OF KILLER ROBOT MUTANTS.
SO, ME AND RED ARE RUNNING DEFENSE?
RIGHT. WE NEED YOU TO COVER US. BLOW DONNIE'S CAPSULE IF THINGS GO WRONG AND WE GET TURNED.
SPEAKING OF... I KNOW YOU'RE IMMUNE TO MUTAGEN, APRIL, BUT YOU'RE STILL PART MUTANT.
IS THERE ANY CHANCE YOU'VE GOT, *UH*, ROBO-POTENTIAL?
I'M SURE I'LL BE FINE. EVEN IF I GOT INFECTED, MY PSYCHIC POWERS WOULD—
I'VE GOT A HIT! STOCKMAN'S NANOBOTS DETECTED TWO BLOCKS EAST!

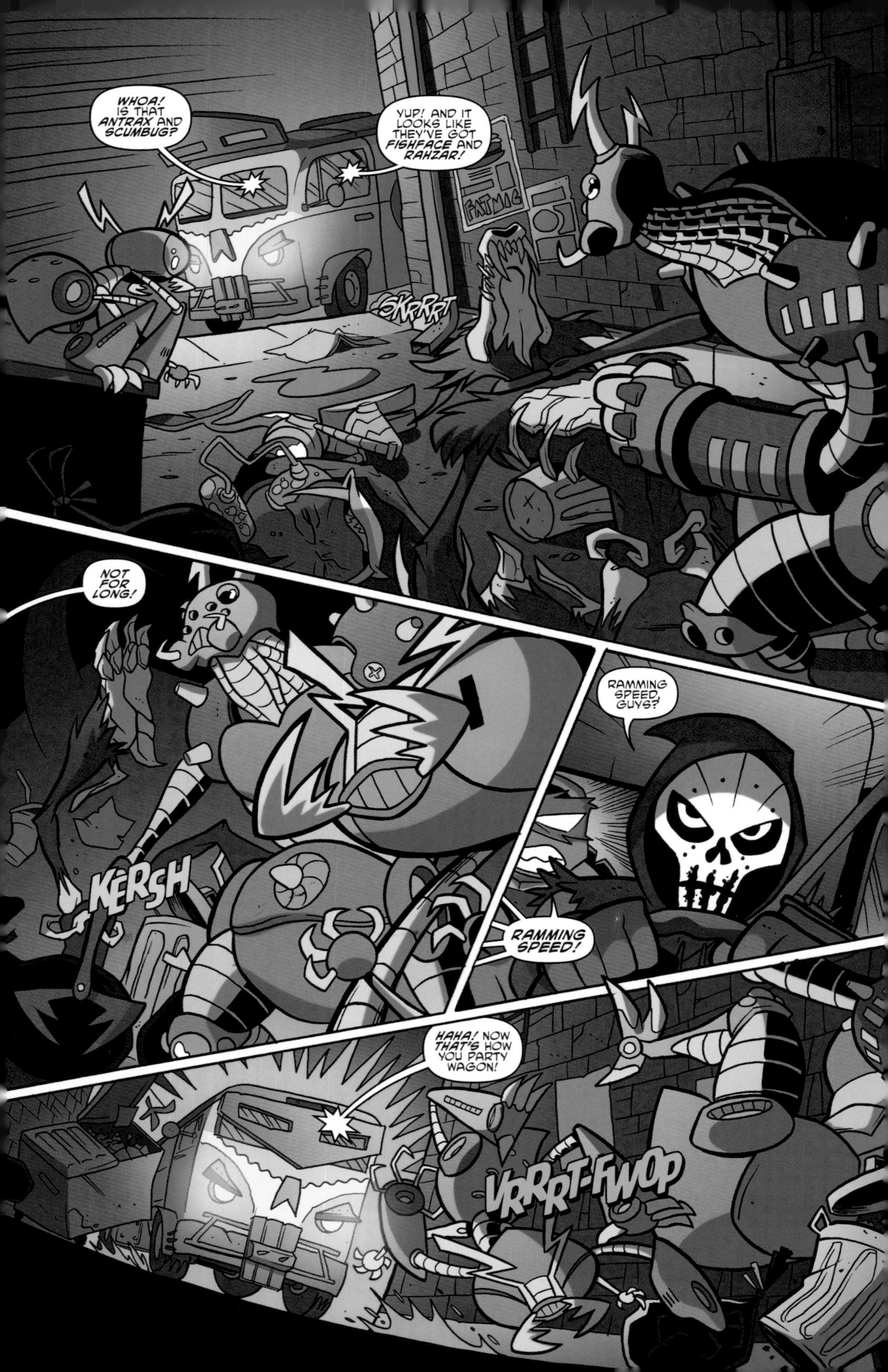
WHOA! IS THAT ANTRAX AND SCUMBUG?
YUP! AND IT LOOKS LIKE THEY'VE GOT FISHFACE AND RAHZAR!
FAT MIC
SKRRRT
NOT FOR LONG!
KERSH
RAMMING SPEED, GUYS?
RAMMING SPEED!
HAHA! NOW THAT'S HOW YOU PARTY WAGON!
VRRRT-FWOP

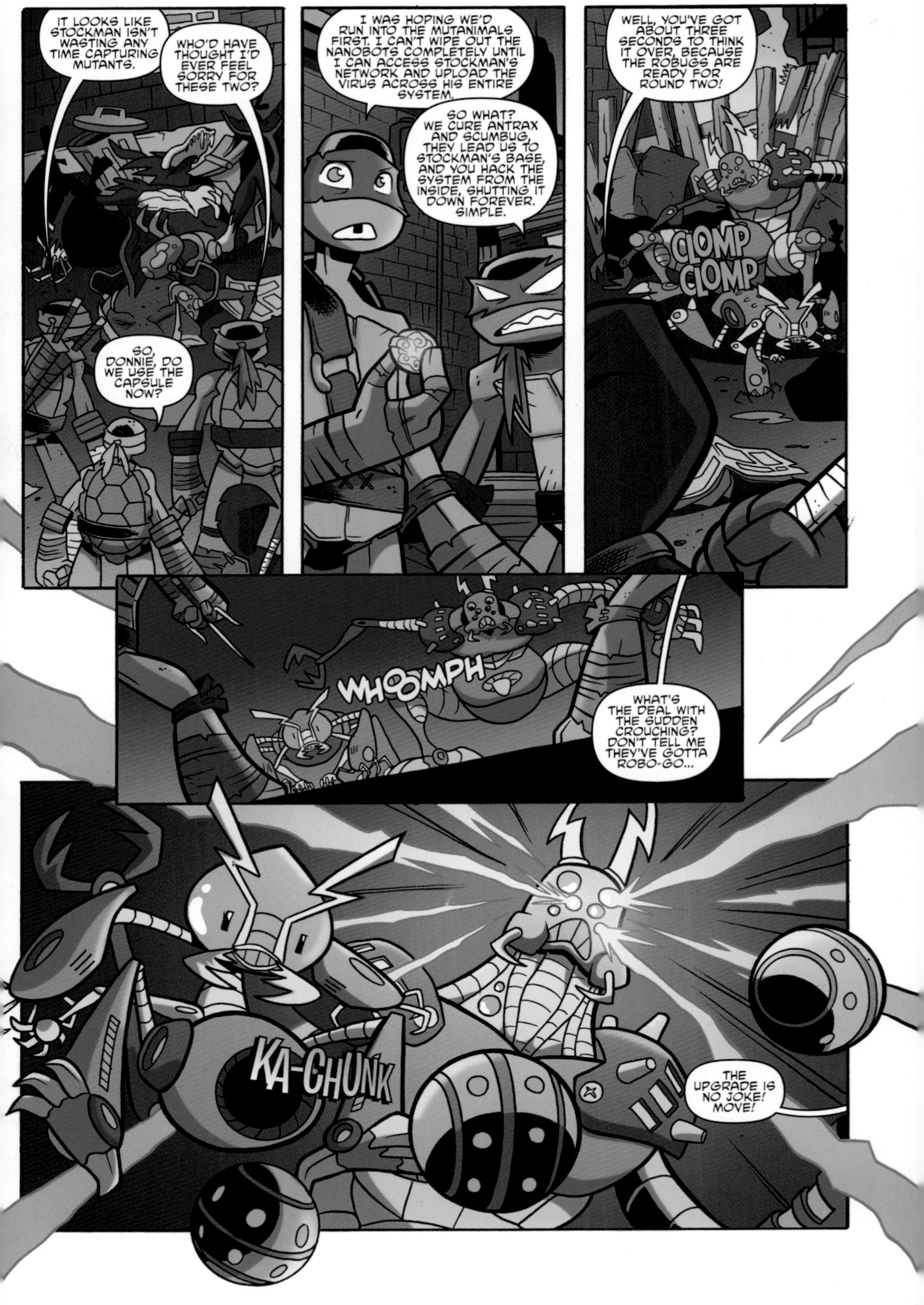
IT LOOKS LIKE STOCKMAN ISN'T WASTING ANY TIME CAPTURING MUTANTS.
WHO'D HAVE THOUGHT I'D EVER FEEL SORRY FOR THESE TWO?
SO, DONNIE, DO WE USE THE CAPSULE NOW?
I WAS HOPING WE'D RUN INTO THE MUTANIMALS FIRST. I CAN'T WIPE OUT THE NANOBOTS COMPLETELY UNTIL I CAN ACCESS STOCKMAN'S NETWORK AND UPLOAD THE VIRUS ACROSS HIS ENTIRE SYSTEM.
SO WHAT? WE CURE ANTRAX AND SCUMBUG, THEY LEAD US TO STOCKMAN'S BASE, AND YOU HACK THE SYSTEM FROM THE INSIDE, SHUTTING IT DOWN FOREVER. SIMPLE.
WELL, YOU'VE GOT ABOUT THREE SECONDS TO THINK IT OVER, BECAUSE THE ROBUGS ARE READY FOR ROUND TWO!
CLOMP CLOMP
WHOOMPH
WHAT'S THE DEAL WITH THE SUDDEN CROUCHING? DON'T TELL ME THEY'VE GOTTA ROBO-GO...
KA-CHUNK
THE UPGRADE IS NO JOKE! MOVE!

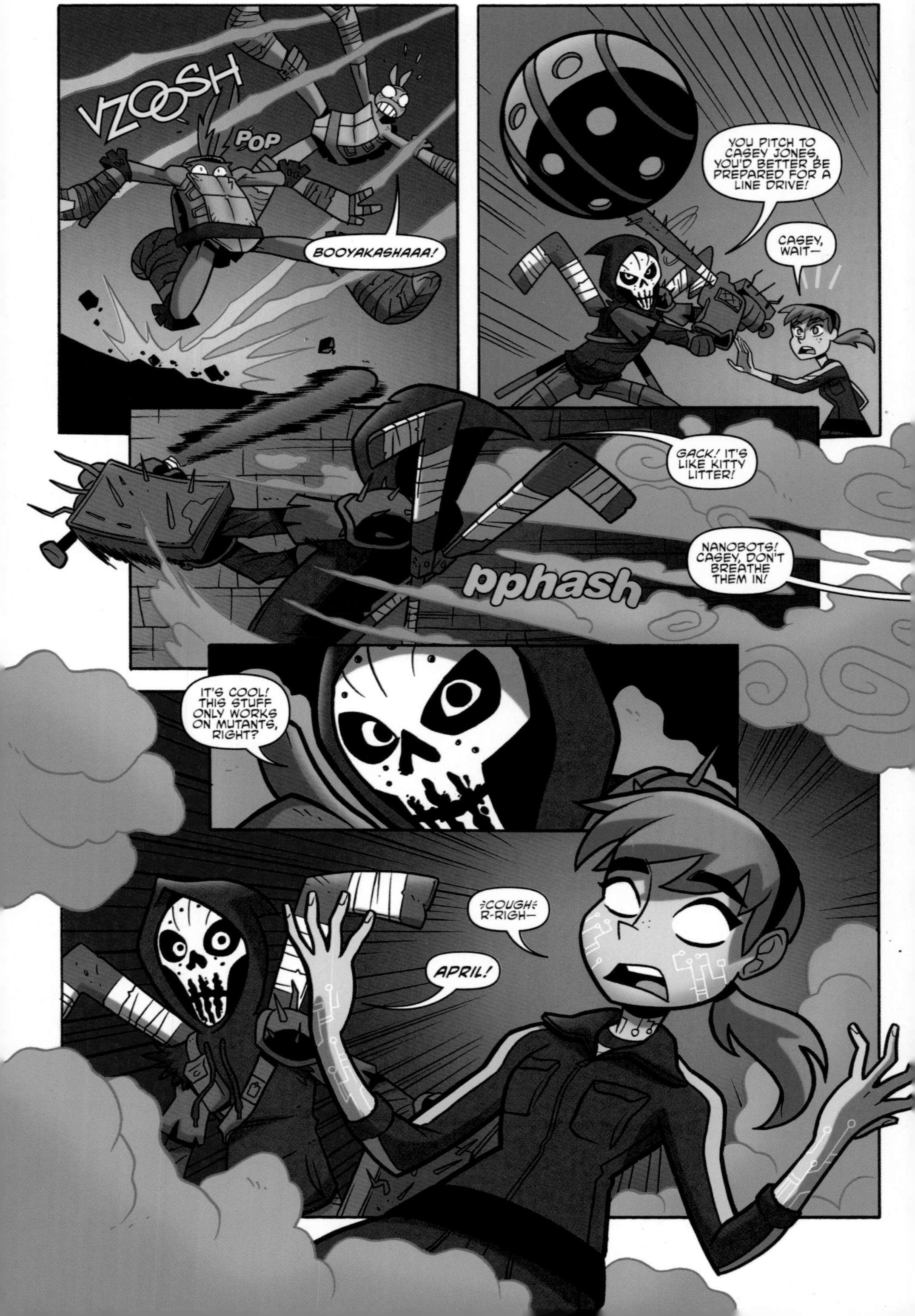
VZOOSH
POP
BOOYAKASHAAA!
YOU PITCH TO CASEY JONES, YOU'D BETTER BE PREPARED FOR A LINE DRIVE!
CASEY, WAIT—
GACK! IT'S LIKE KITTY LITTER!
NANOBOTS! CASEY, DON'T BREATHE THEM IN!
pphash
IT'S COOL! THIS STUFF ONLY WORKS ON MUTANTS, RIGHT?
COUGH R-RIGH—
APRIL!

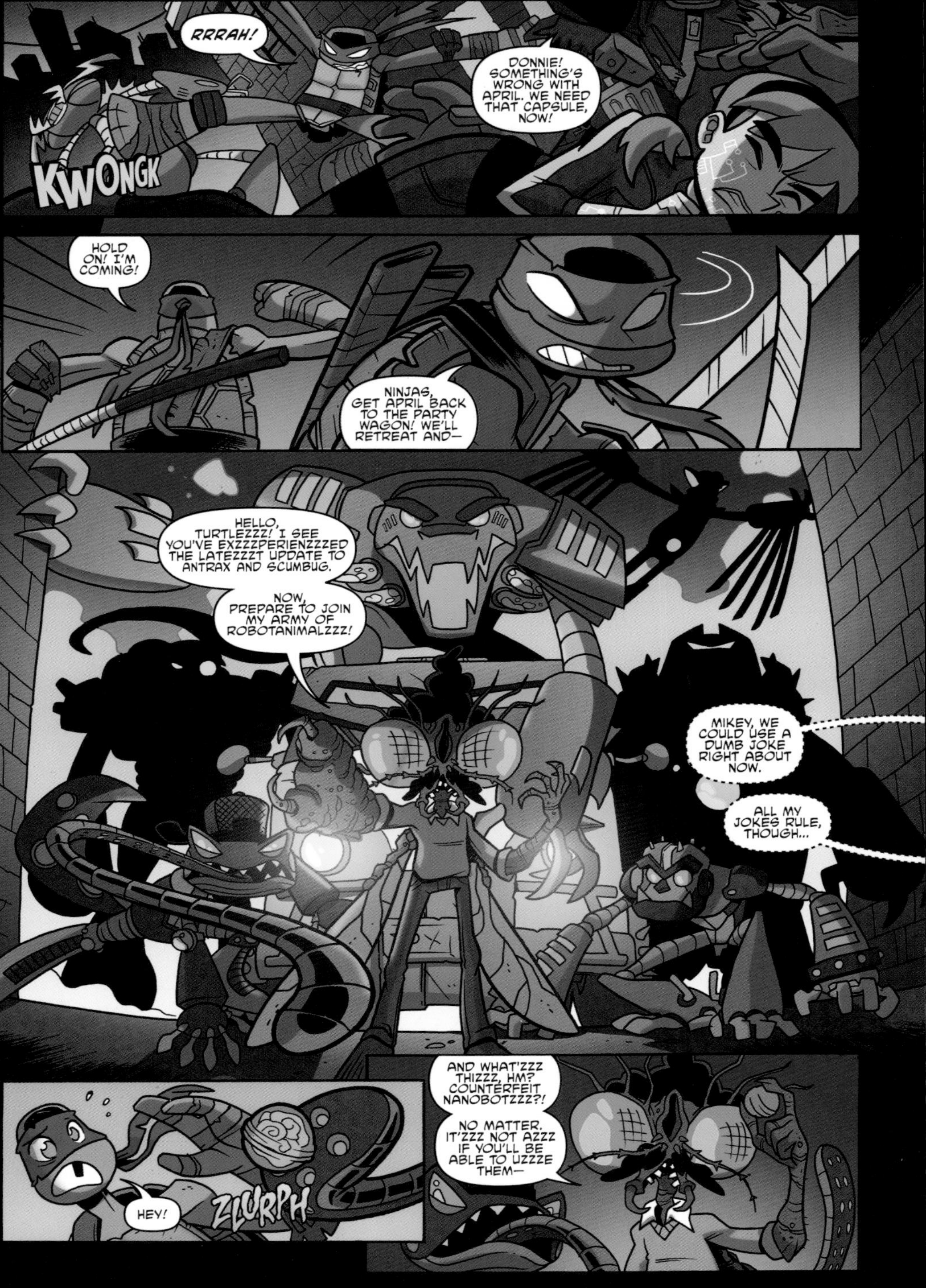
RRRAH!
DONNIE! SOMETHING'S WRONG WITH APRIL. WE NEED THAT CAPSULE, NOW!
KWONGK
HOLD ON! I'M COMING!
NINJAS, GET APRIL BACK TO THE PARTY WAGON! WE'LL RETREAT AND—
HELLO, TURTLEZZZ! I SEE YOU'VE EXZZZPERIENZZZED THE LATEZZZT UPDATE TO ANTRAX AND SCUMBUG.
NOW, PREPARE TO JOIN MY ARMY OF ROBOTANIMALZZZ!
MIKEY, WE COULD USE A DUMB JOKE RIGHT ABOUT NOW.
ALL MY JOKES RULE, THOUGH...
HEY!
ZLURPH
AND WHAT'ZZZ THIZZZ, HM? COUNTERFEIT NANOBOTZZZ?!
NO MATTER. IT'ZZZ NOT AZZZ IF YOU'LL BE ABLE TO UZZZE THEM—

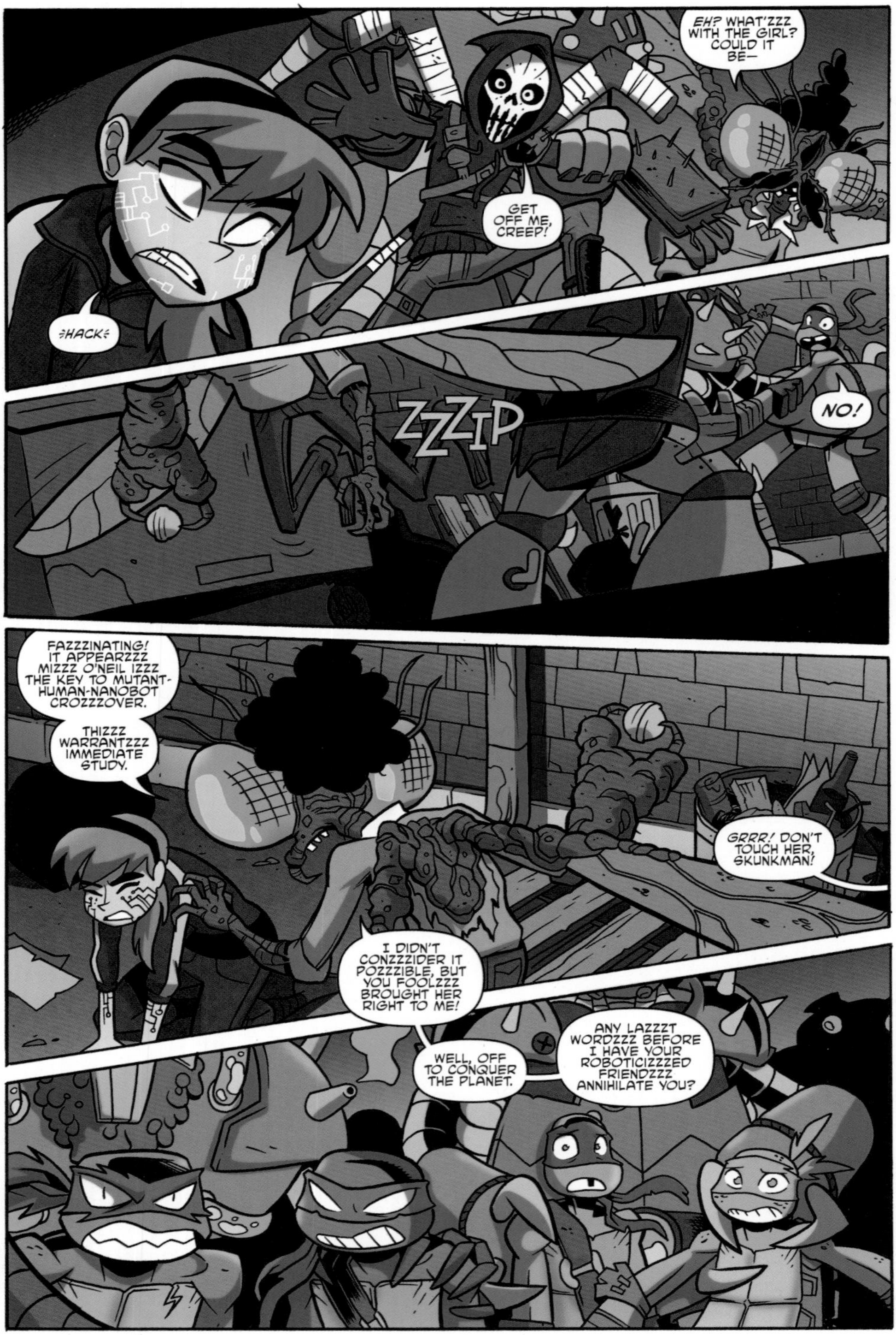
EH? WHAT'ZZZ WITH THE GIRL? COULD IT BE—
GET OFF ME, CREEP!
HACK
ZZZIP
NO!
FAZZZINATING! IT APPEARZZZ MIZZZ O'NEIL IZZZ THE KEY TO MUTANT-HUMAN-NANOBOT CROZZZOVER.
THIZZZ WARRANTZZZ IMMEDIATE STUDY.
GRRR! DON'T TOUCH HER, SKUNKMAN!
I DIDN'T CONZZZIDER IT POZZZIBLE, BUT YOU FOOLZZZ BROUGHT HER RIGHT TO ME!
WELL, OFF TO CONQUER THE PLANET.
ANY LAZZZT WORDZZZ BEFORE I HAVE YOUR ROBOTICIZZZED FRIENDZZZ ANNIHILATE YOU?

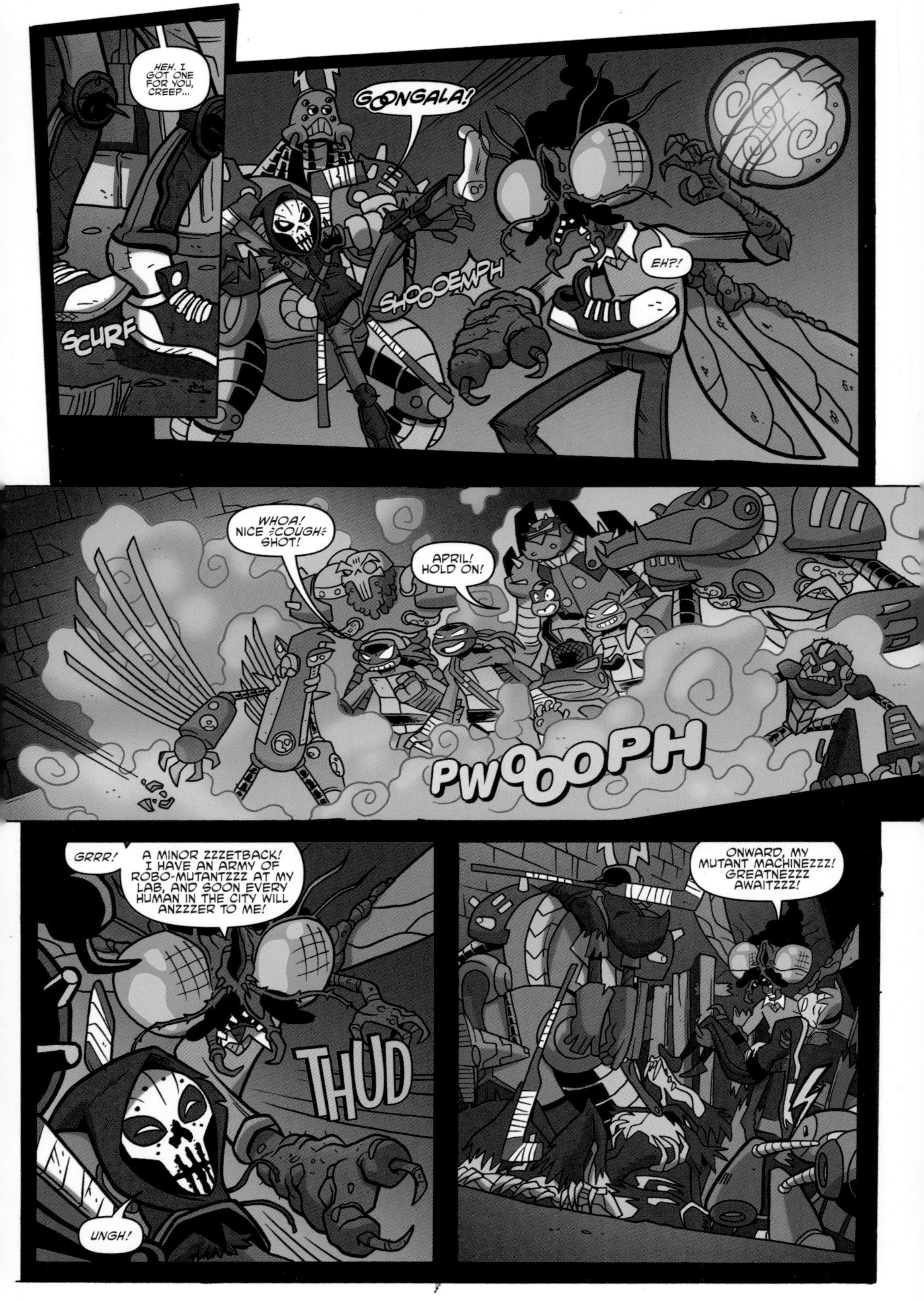
HEH. I GOT ONE FOR YOU, CREEP...
SCURF
GOONGALA!
SHOOOEMPH
EH?!
WHOA! NICE =COUGH= SHOT!
APRIL! HOLD ON!
PWOOOOPH
GRRR!
A MINOR ZZZETBACK! I HAVE AN ARMY OF ROBO-MUTANTZZZ AT MY LAB, AND SOON EVERY HUMAN IN THE CITY WILL ANZZZER TO ME!
THUD
UNGH!
ONWARD, MY MUTANT MACHINEZZZ! GREATNEZZZ AWAITZZZ!

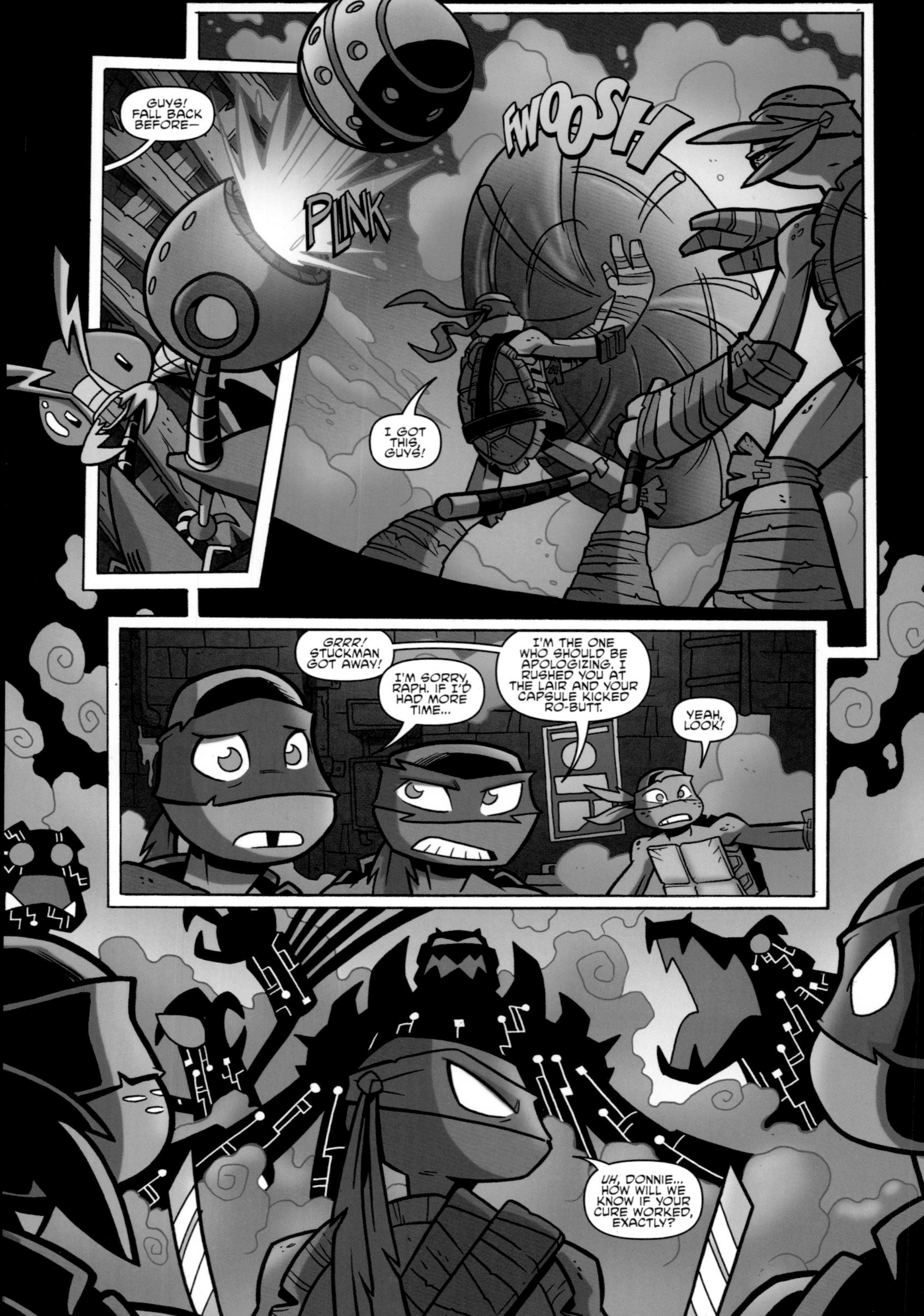

GUYS! FALL BACK BEFORE—
FWOOSH
PLINK
I GOT THIS, GUYS!
GRRR! STUCKMAN GOT AWAY!
I'M SORRY, RAPH. IF I'D HAD MORE TIME...
I'M THE ONE WHO SHOULD BE APOLOGIZING. I RUSHED YOU AT THE LAIR AND YOUR CAPSULE KICKED RO-BUTT.
YEAH, LOOK!
UH, DONNIE... HOW WILL WE KNOW IF YOUR CURE WORKED, EXACTLY?

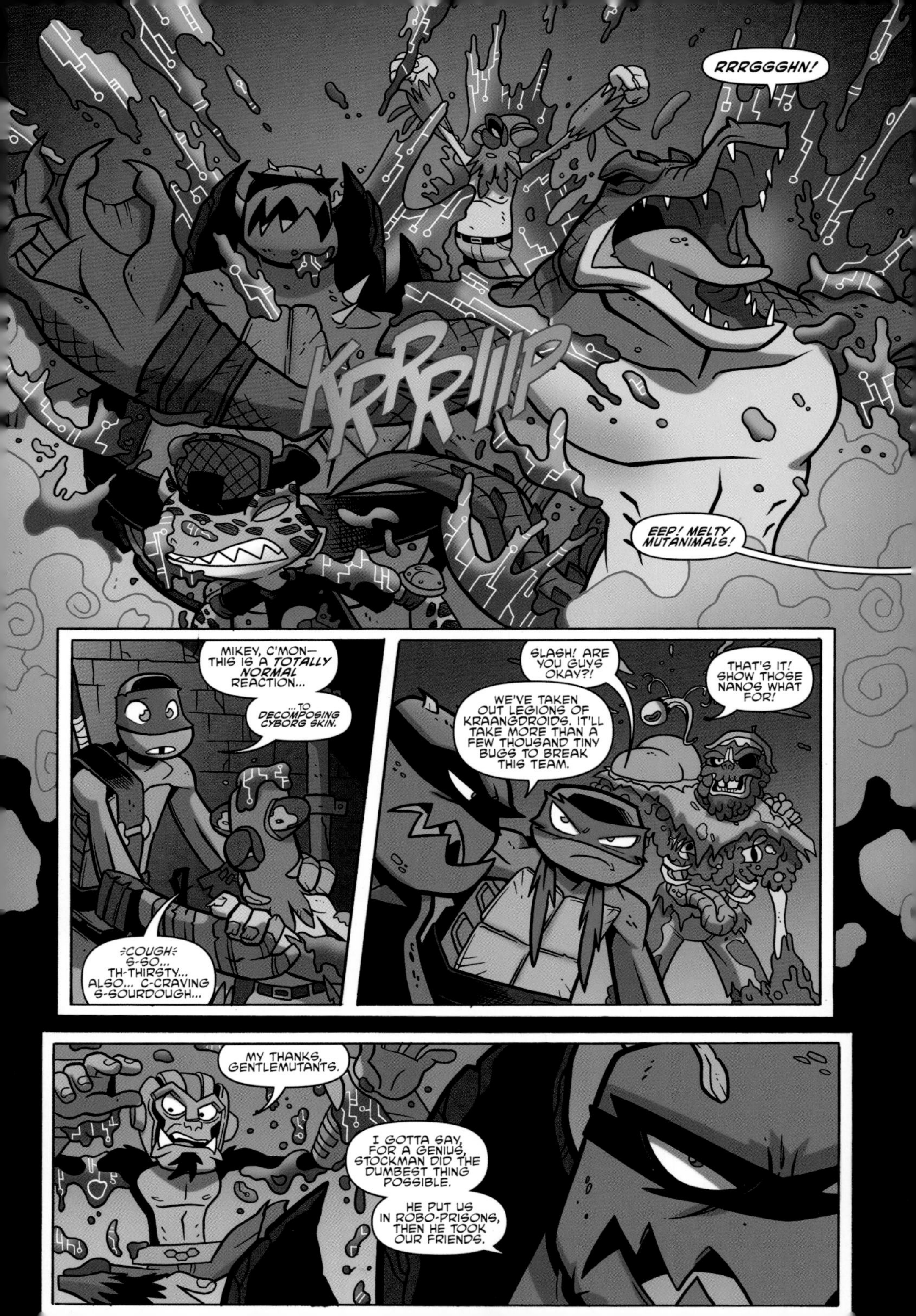
RRRGGGHN!
KRRRIIIP
EEP! MELTY MUTANIMALS!
MIKEY, C'MON— THIS IS A *TOTALLY NORMAL* REACTION...
...TO *DECOMPOSING CYBORG SKIN.*
≠COUGH≠ S-SO... TH-THIRSTY... ALSO... C-CRAVING S-SOURDOUGH...
SLASH! ARE YOU GUYS OKAY?!
WE'VE TAKEN OUT LEGIONS OF KRAANGDROIDS. IT'LL TAKE MORE THAN A FEW THOUSAND TINY BUGS TO BREAK THIS TEAM.
THAT'S IT! SHOW THOSE NANOS WHAT FOR!
MY THANKS, GENTLEMUTANTS.
I GOTTA SAY, FOR A GENIUS, STOCKMAN DID THE DUMBEST THING POSSIBLE.
HE PUT US IN ROBO-PRISONS, THEN HE TOOK OUR FRIENDS.

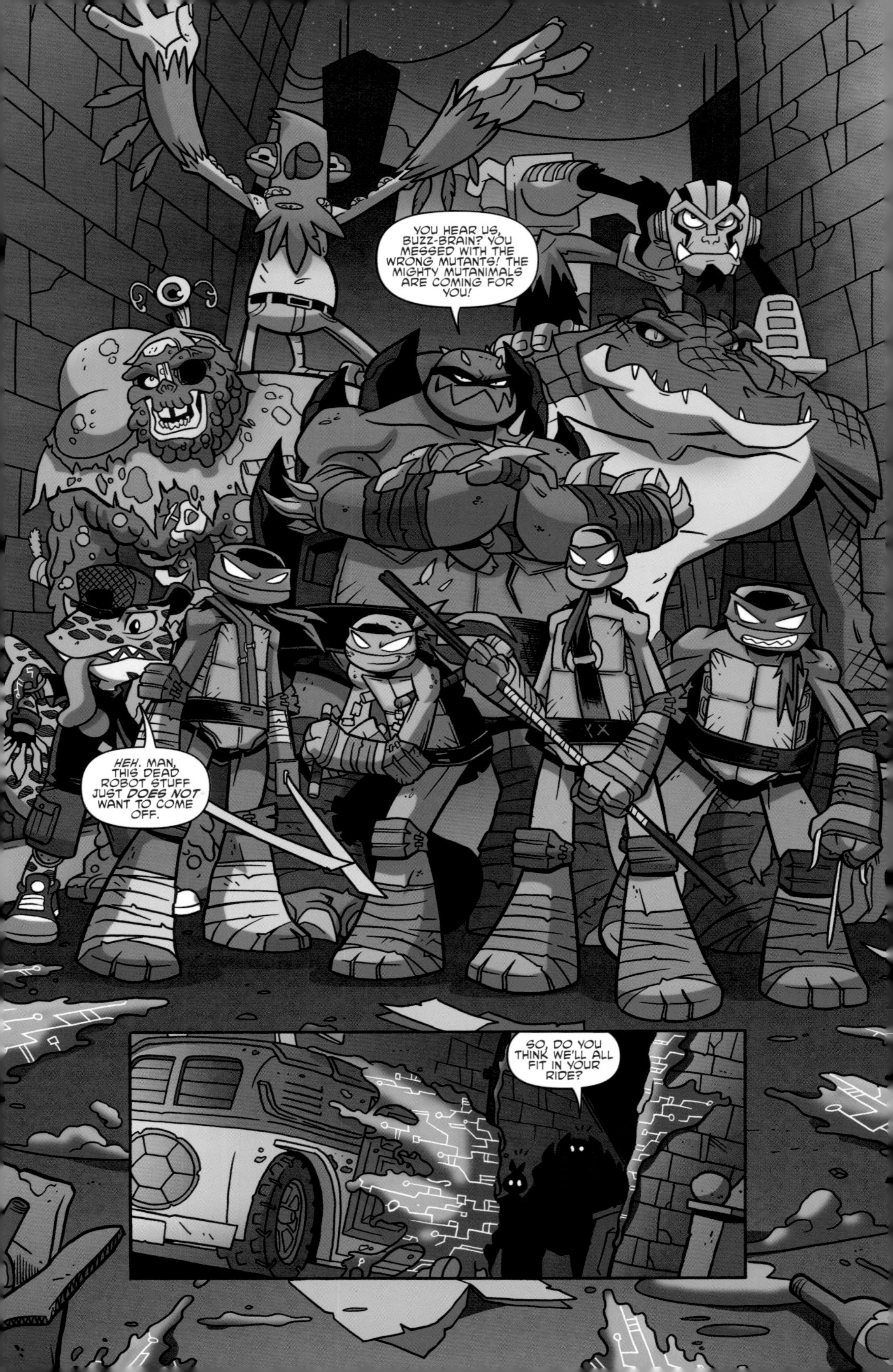
YOU HEAR US, BUZZ-BRAIN? YOU MESSED WITH THE WRONG MUTANTS! THE MIGHTY MUTANIMALS ARE COMING FOR YOU!
HEH. MAN, THIS DEAD ROBOT STUFF JUST DOES NOT WANT TO COME OFF.
SO, DO YOU THINK WE'LL ALL FIT IN YOUR RIDE?

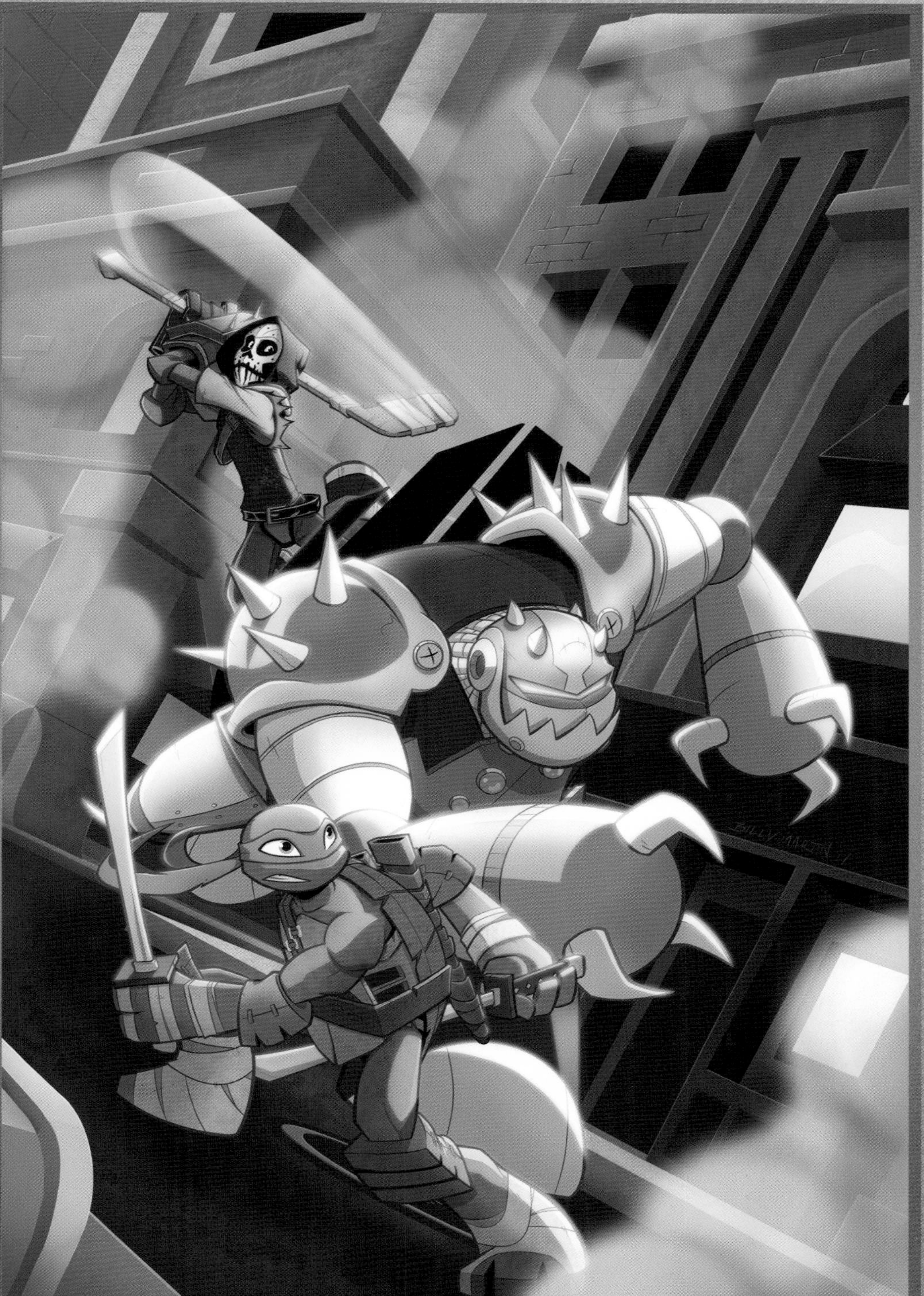

Artist: Billy Martin

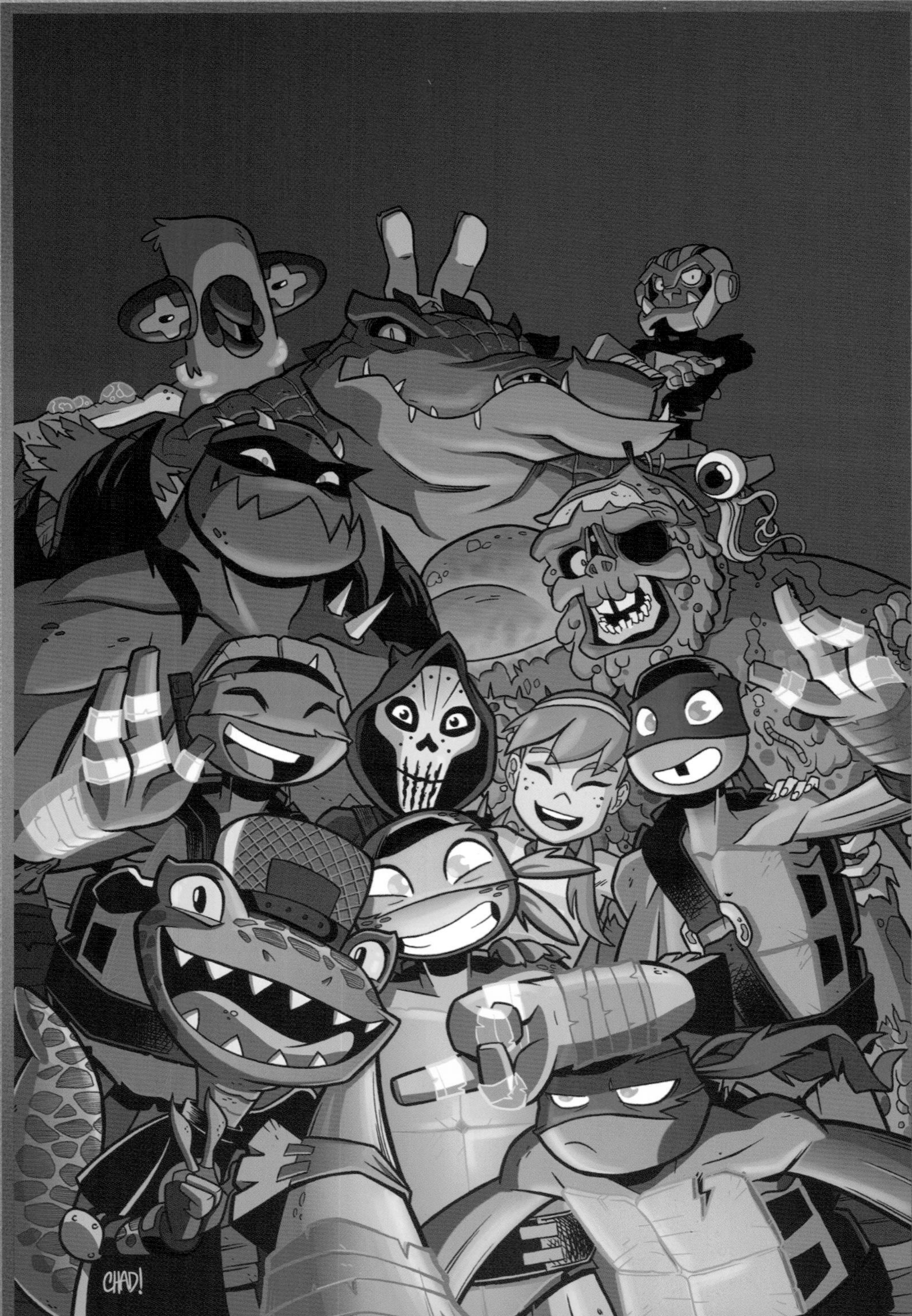
CHAD!

Artist: Chad Thomas

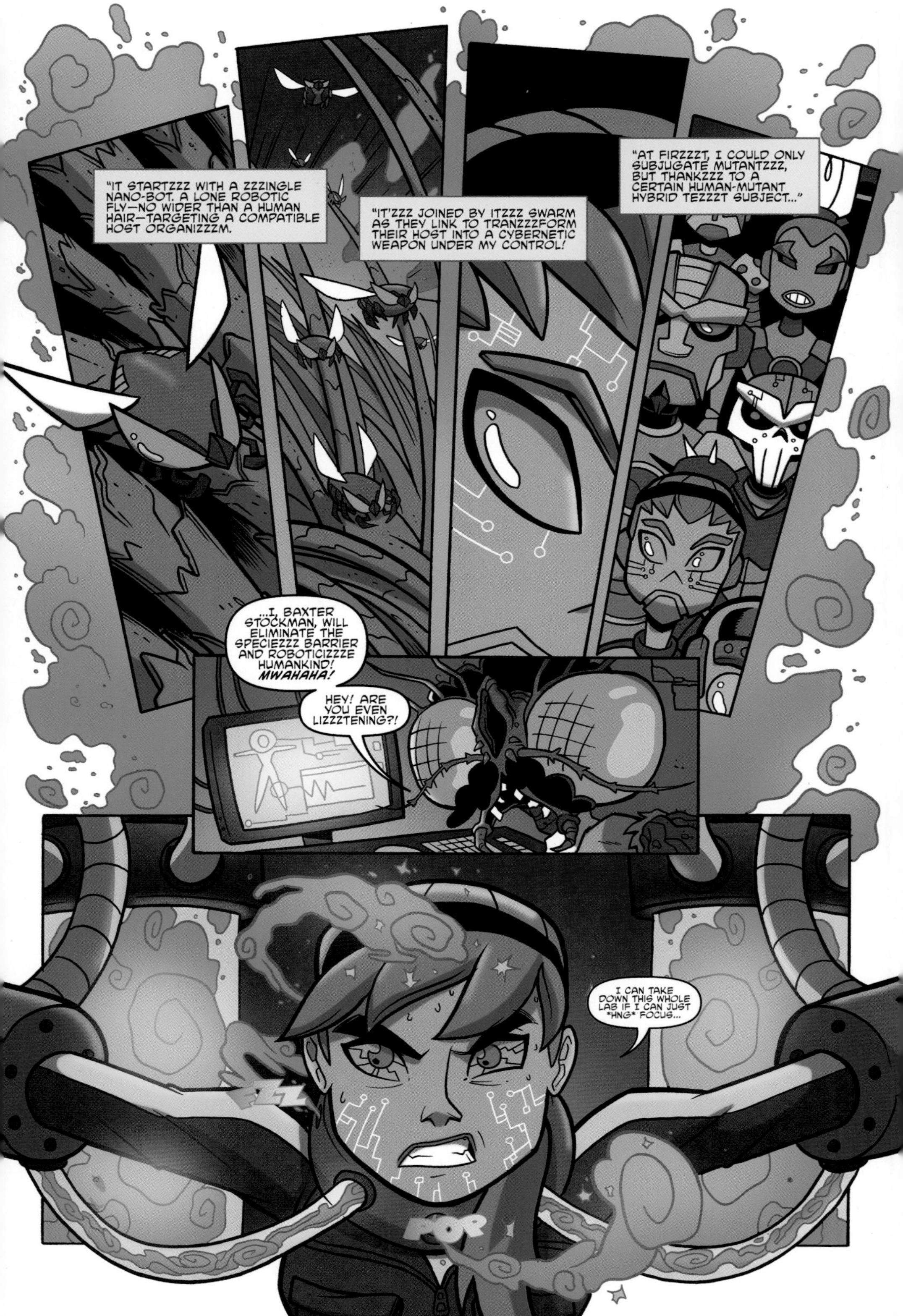
"IT STARTZZZ WITH A ZZZINGLE NANO-BOT. A LONE ROBOTIC FLY—NO WIDER THAN A HUMAN HAIR—TARGETING A COMPATIBLE HOST ORGANIZZZM.
"IT'ZZZ JOINED BY ITZZZ SWARM AS THEY LINK TO TRANZZZFORM THEIR HOST INTO A CYBERNETIC WEAPON UNDER MY CONTROL!
"AT FIRZZZT, I COULD ONLY SUBJUGATE MUTANTZZZ, BUT THANKZZZ TO A CERTAIN HUMAN-MUTANT HYBRID TEZZZT SUBJECT..."
...I, BAXTER STOCKMAN, WILL ELIMINATE THE SPECIEZZZ BARRIER AND ROBOTICIZZZE HUMANKIND! MWAHAHA!
HEY! ARE YOU EVEN LIZZZTENING?!
I CAN TAKE DOWN THIS WHOLE LAB IF I CAN JUST *HNG* FOCUS...
FZZZ
POP

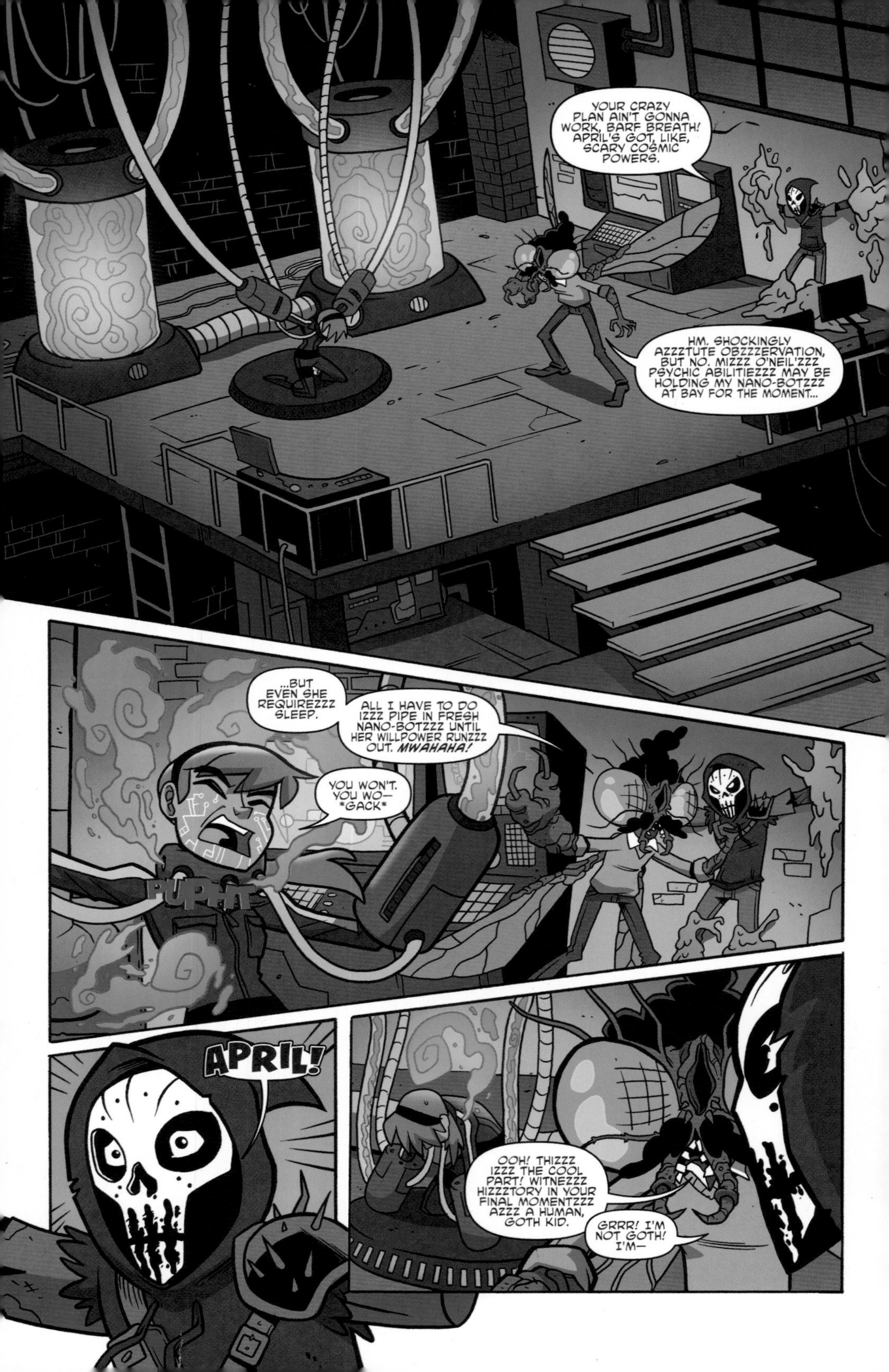

YOUR CRAZY PLAN AIN'T GONNA WORK, BARF BREATH! APRIL'S GOT, LIKE, SCARY COSMIC POWERS.
HM. SHOCKINGLY AZZZTUTE OBZZZERVATION, BUT NO. MIZZZ O'NEIL'ZZZ PSYCHIC ABILITIEZZZ MAY BE HOLDING MY NANO-BOTZZZ AT BAY FOR THE MOMENT...
...BUT EVEN SHE REQUIREZZZ SLEEP.
ALL I HAVE TO DO IZZZ PIPE IN FRESH NANO-BOTZZZ UNTIL HER WILLPOWER RUNZZZ OUT. *MWAHAHA!*
YOU WON'T. YOU WO— *GACK*
PUPHT
APRIL!
OOH! THIZZZ IZZZ THE COOL PART! WITNEZZZ HIZZZTORY IN YOUR FINAL MOMENTZZZ AZZZ A HUMAN, GOTH KID.
GRRR! I'M NOT GOTH! I'M—

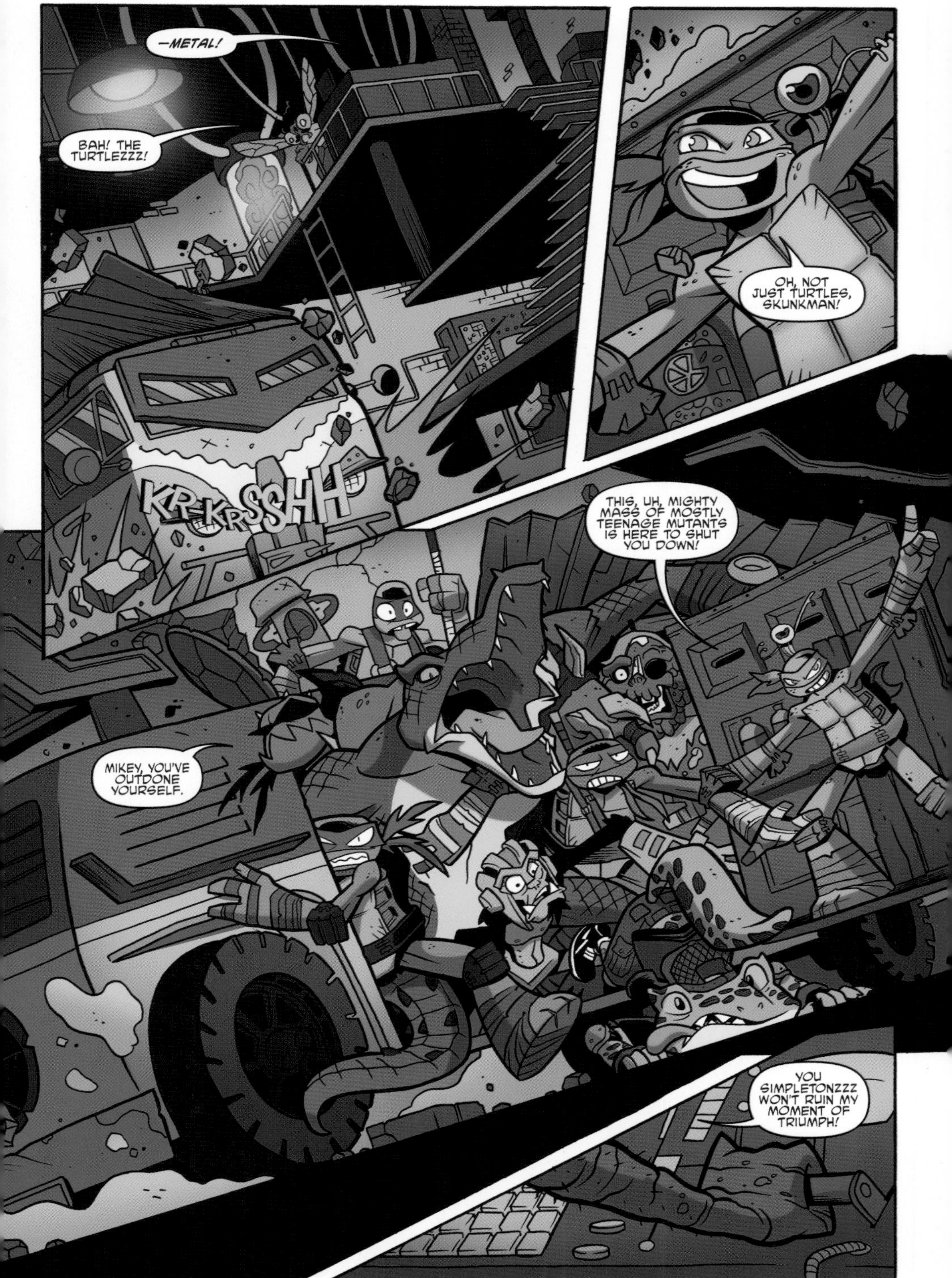
—METAL!
BAH! THE TURTLEZZZ!
KR-KR-KRSSHH
OH, NOT JUST TURTLES, SKUNKMAN!
THIS, UH, MIGHTY MASS OF MOSTLY TEENAGE MUTANTS IS HERE TO SHUT YOU DOWN!
MIKEY, YOU'VE OUTDONE YOURSELF.
YOU SIMPLETONZZZ WON'T RUIN MY MOMENT OF TRIUMPH!

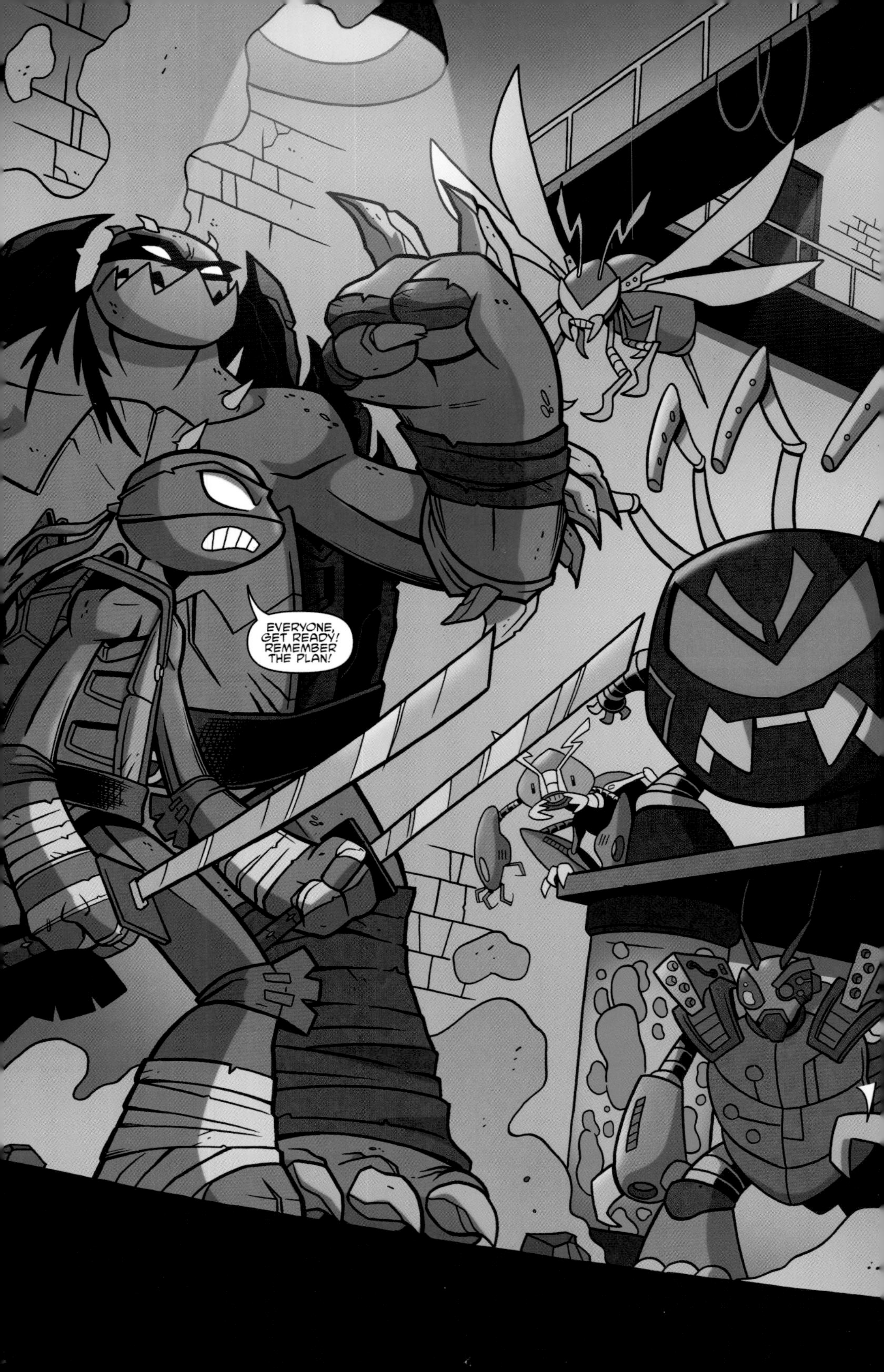
EVERYONE, GET READY! REMEMBER THE PLAN!

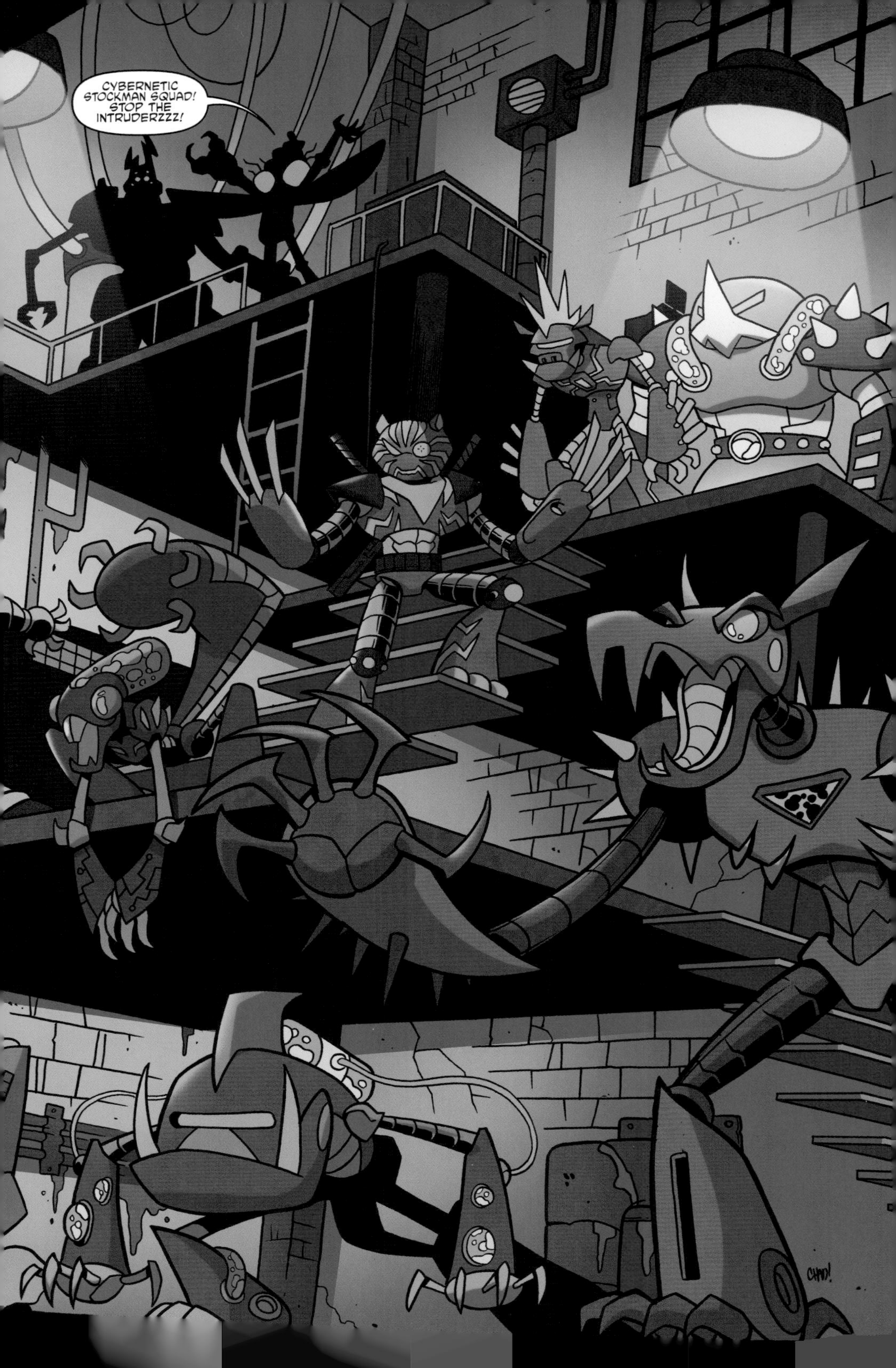
CYBERNETIC STOCKMAN SQUAD! STOP THE INTRUDERZZZ!
CHAD!

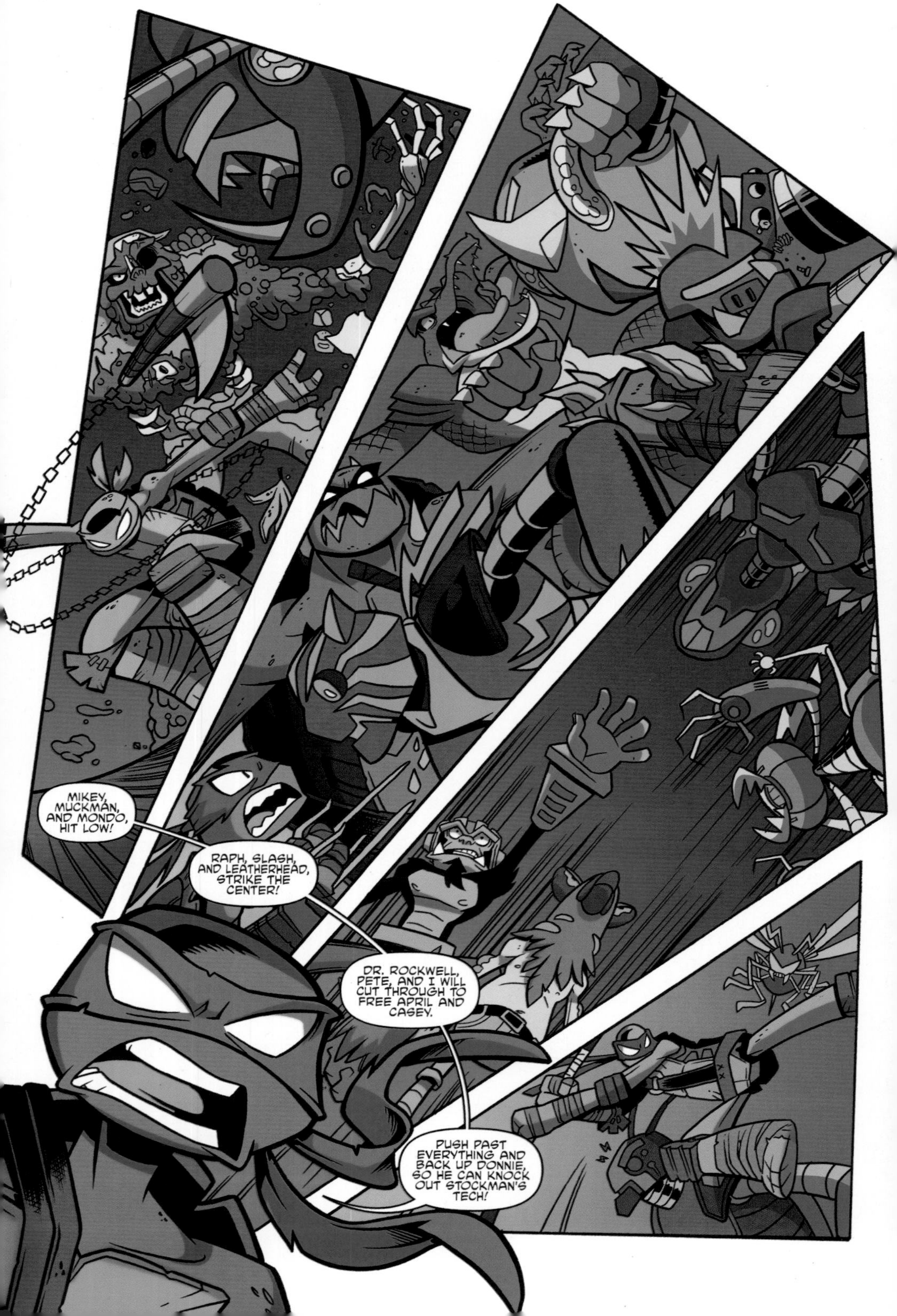
MIKEY, MUCKMAN, AND MONDO, HIT LOW!
RAPH, SLASH, AND LEATHERHEAD, STRIKE THE CENTER!
DR. ROCKWELL, PETE, AND I WILL CUT THROUGH TO FREE APRIL AND CASEY.
PUSH PAST EVERYTHING AND BACK UP DONNIE, SO HE CAN KNOCK OUT STOCKMAN'S TECH!

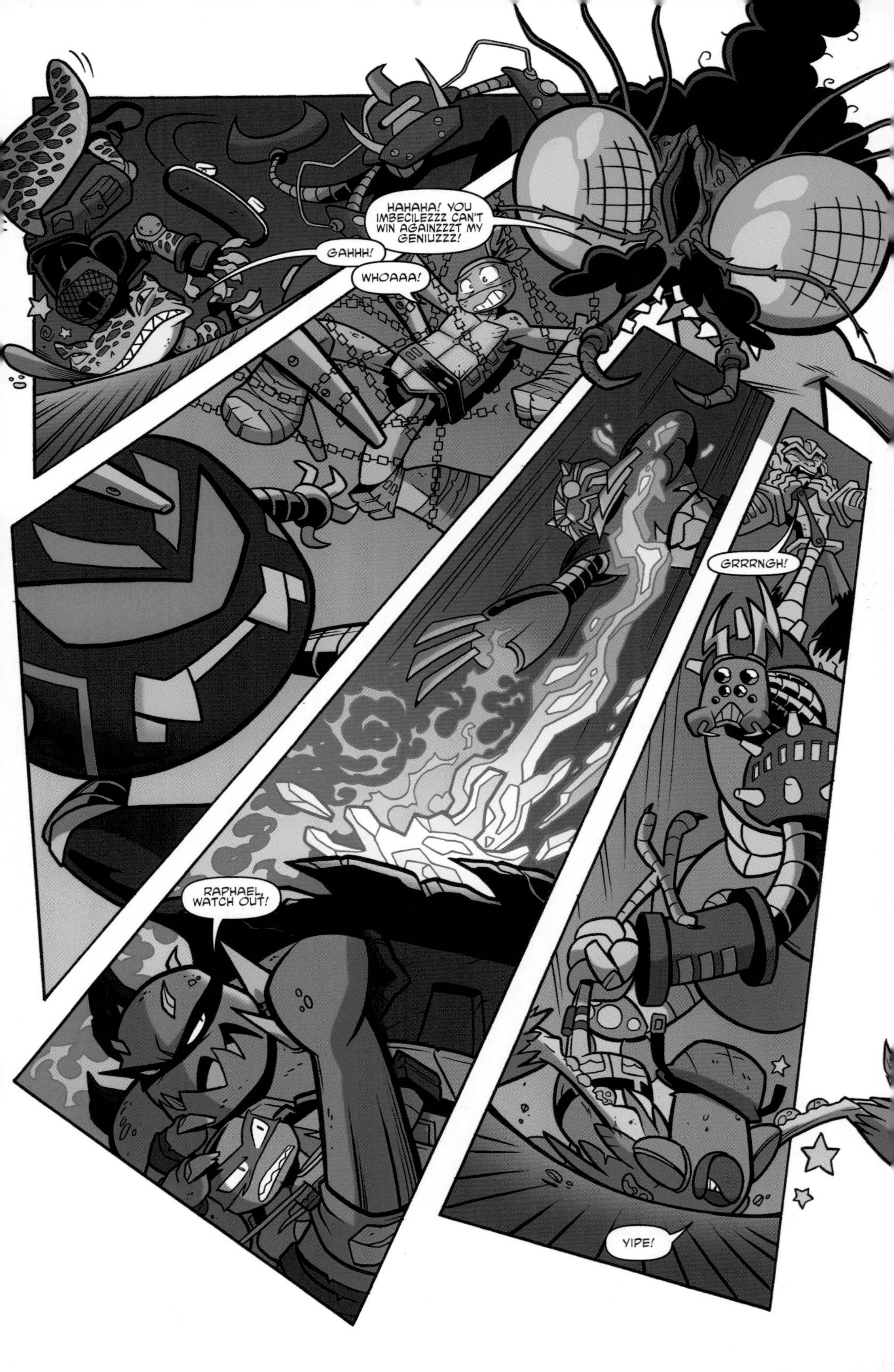
HAHAHA! YOU IMBECILEZZZ CAN'T WIN AGAINZZZT MY GENIUZZZ!
GAHHH!
WHOAAA!
GRRRNGH!
RAPHAEL, WATCH OUT!
YIPE!

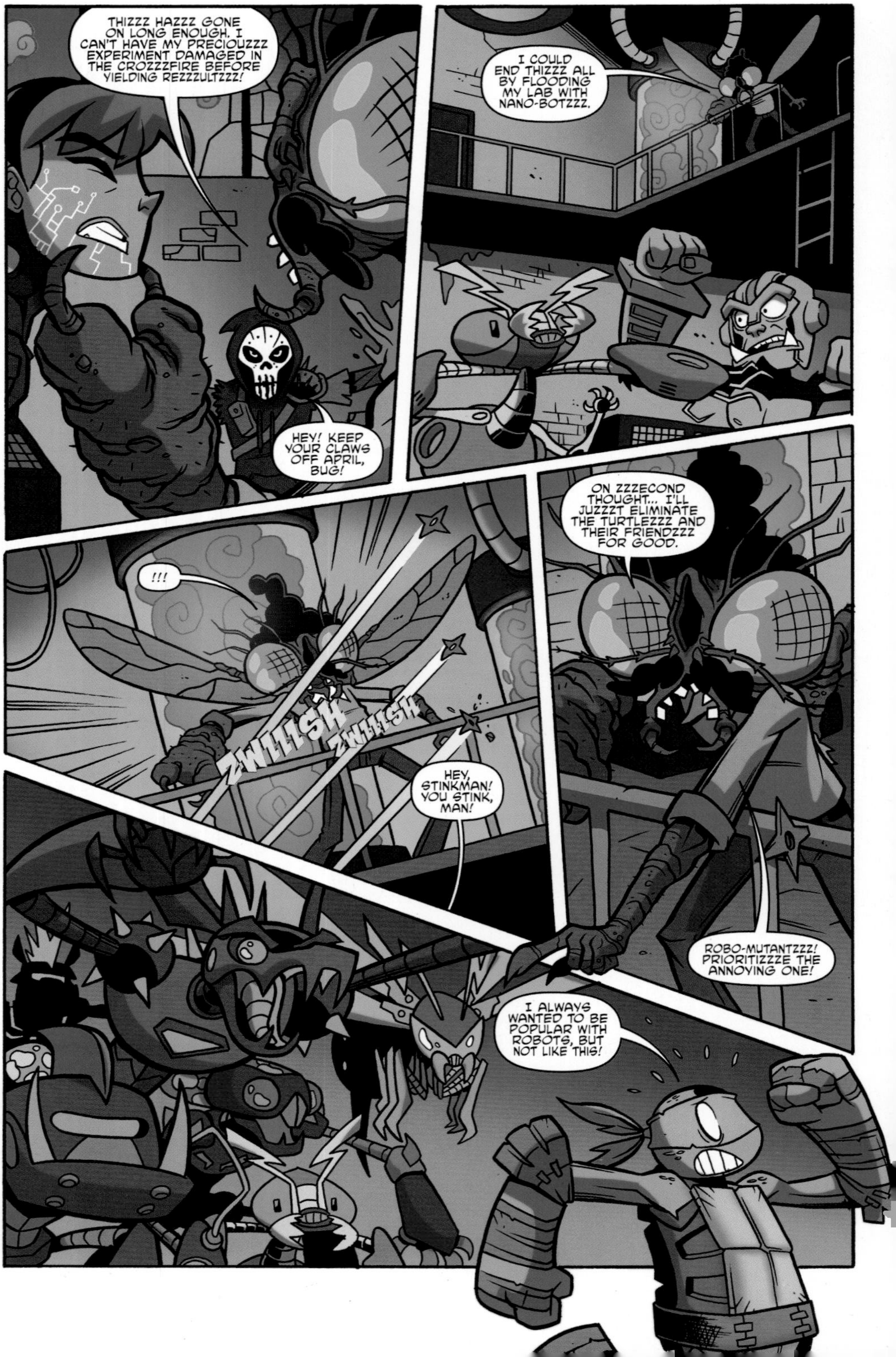
THIZZZ HAZZZ GONE ON LONG ENOUGH. I CAN'T HAVE MY PRECIOUZZZ EXPERIMENT DAMAGED IN THE CROZZZFIRE BEFORE YIELDING REZZZULTZZZ!
HEY! KEEP YOUR CLAWS OFF APRIL, BUG!
I COULD END THIZZZ ALL BY FLOODING MY LAB WITH NANO-BOTZZZ.
ON ZZZECOND THOUGHT... I'LL JUZZZT ELIMINATE THE TURTLEZZZ AND THEIR FRIENDZZZ FOR GOOD.
!!!
ZWIIISH
ZWIIISH
HEY, STINKMAN! YOU STINK, MAN!
ROBO-MUTANTZZZ! PRIORITIZZZE THE ANNOYING ONE!
I ALWAYS WANTED TO BE POPULAR WITH ROBOTS, BUT NOT LIKE THIS!

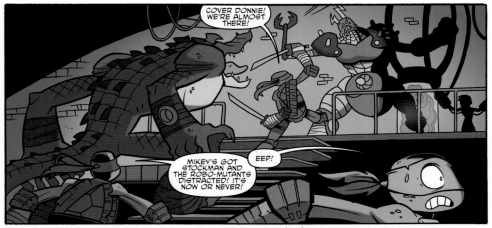

COVER DONNIE! WE'RE ALMOST THERE!

MIKEY'S GOT STOCKMAN AND THE ROBO-MUTANTS DISTRACTED! IT'S NOW OR NEVER!

EEP!

RRRAH!

OUR WINDOW IS CLOSING!

REZZZIZZZTANCE IZZZ FUTILE!

YOU'RE OUT OF COUNTERFEIT NANO-BOTZZZ, AND YOU CAN'T POZZZIBLY DEFEAT MY INVINZZZIBLE ROBOTICIZZZED MUTANTZZZ!

HEH. WE DON'T NEED TO. I JUST REPROGRAMMED YOUR ENTIRE NANO-BOT SWARM...

... AND THEY'RE STARVING.

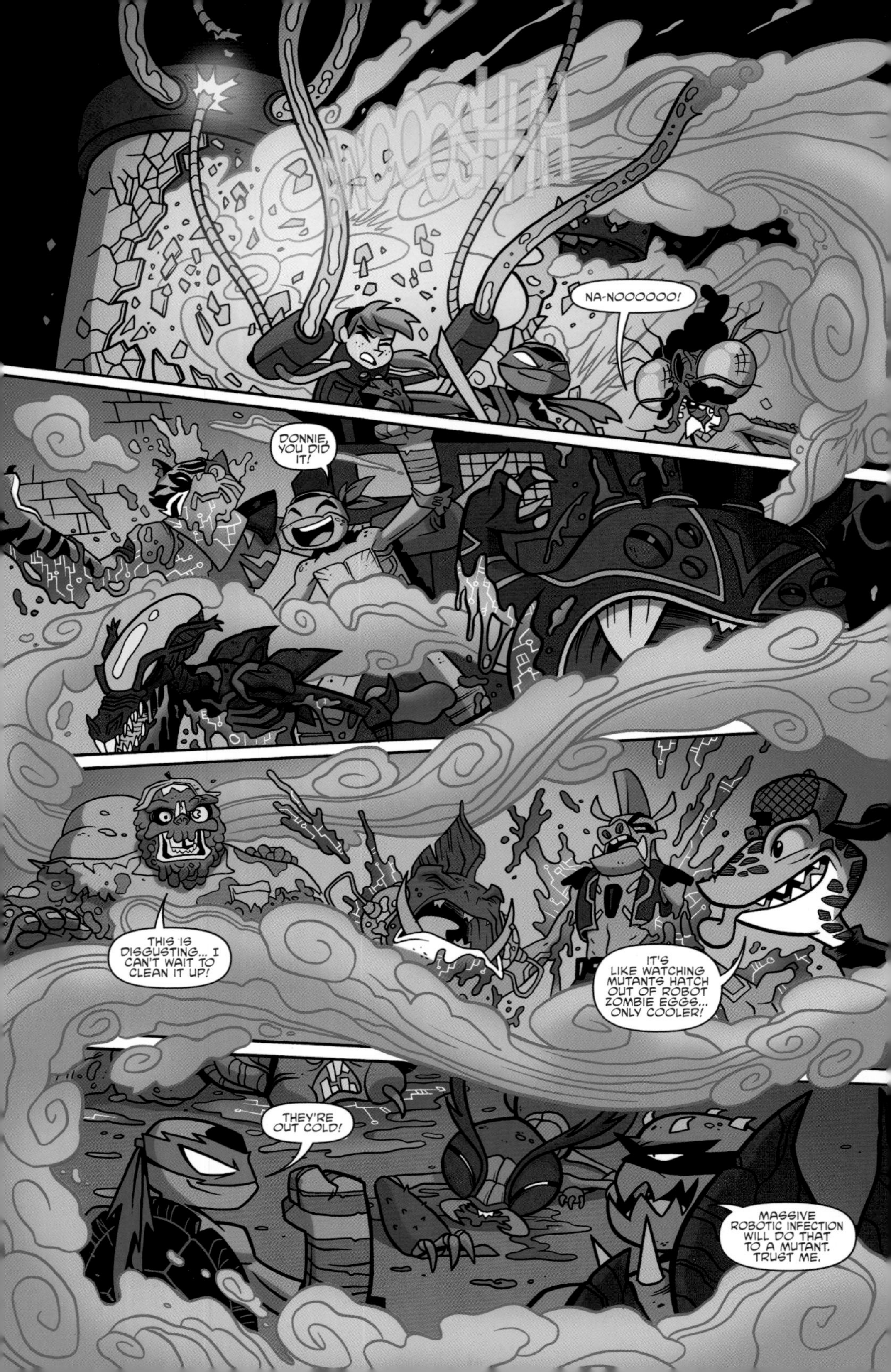
NA-NOOOOOO!
DONNIE, YOU DID IT!
THIS IS DISGUSTING... I CAN'T WAIT TO CLEAN IT UP!
IT'S LIKE WATCHING MUTANTS HATCH OUT OF ROBOT ZOMBIE EGGS... ONLY COOLER!
THEY'RE OUT COLD!
MASSIVE ROBOTIC INFECTION WILL DO THAT TO A MUTANT. TRUST ME.

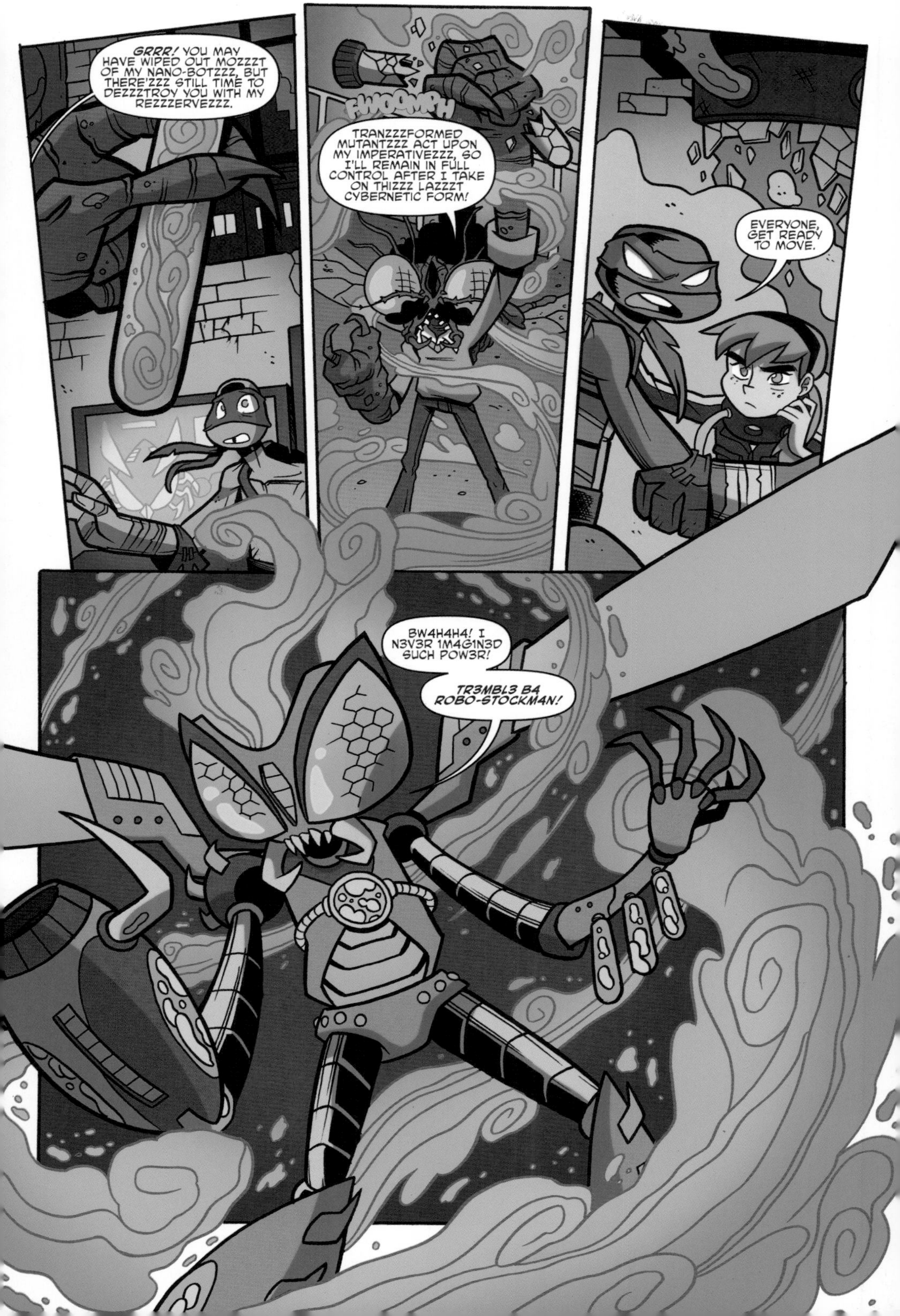
GRRR! YOU MAY HAVE WIPED OUT MOZZZT OF MY NANO-BOTZZZ, BUT THERE'ZZZ STILL TIME TO DEZZZTROY YOU WITH MY REZZZERVEZZZ.
FWOOMPH
TRANZZZFORMED MUTANTZZZ ACT UPON MY IMPERATIVEZZZ, SO I'LL REMAIN IN FULL CONTROL AFTER I TAKE ON THIZZZ LAZZZT CYBERNETIC FORM!
EVERYONE, GET READY TO MOVE.
BW4H4H4! I N3V3R 1M4G1N3D SUCH POW3R!
TR3MBL3 B4 ROBO-STOCKM4N!

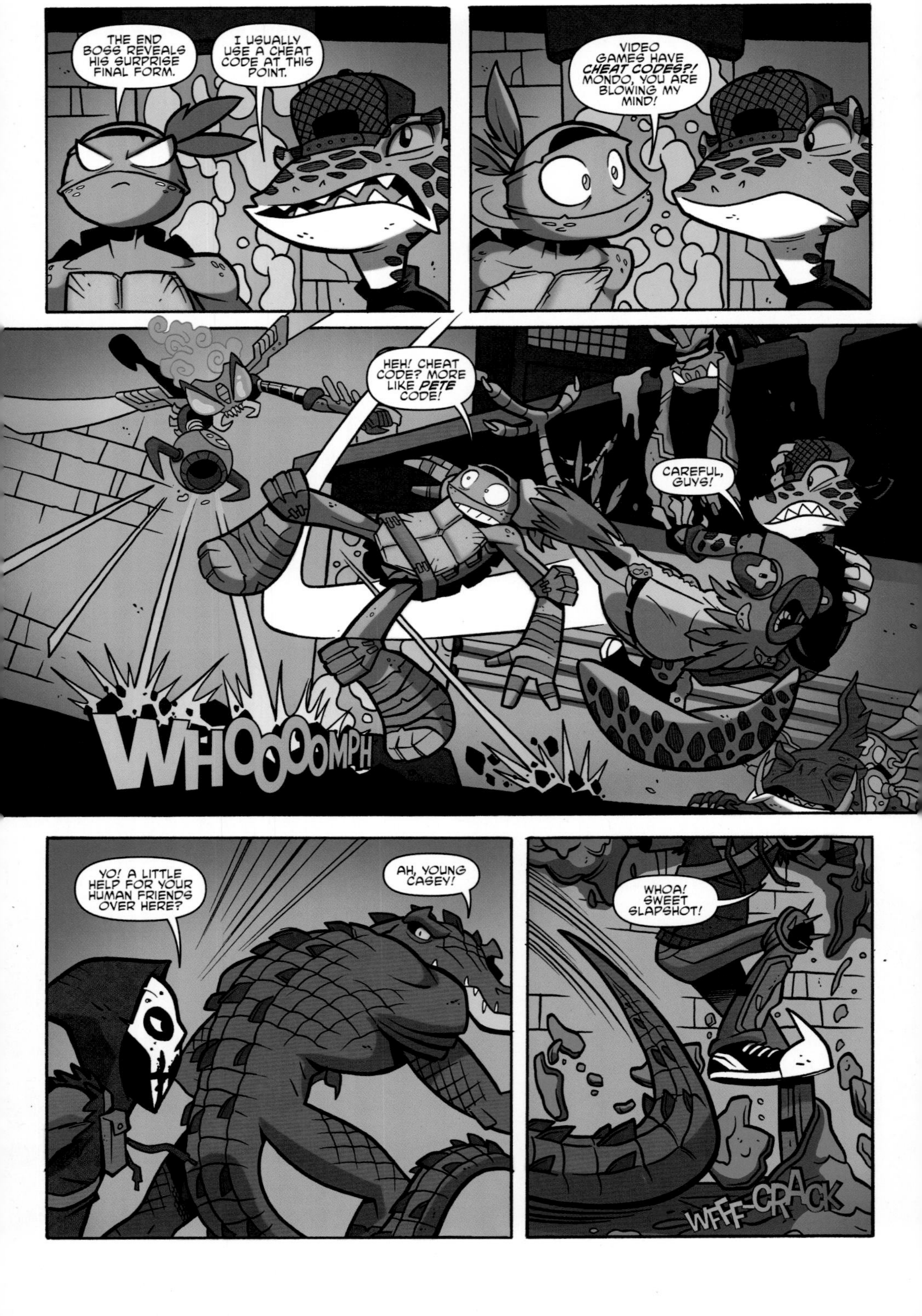
THE END BOSS REVEALS HIS SURPRISE FINAL FORM.
I USUALLY USE A CHEAT CODE AT THIS POINT.
VIDEO GAMES HAVE CHEAT CODES?! MONDO, YOU ARE BLOWING MY MIND!
HEH! CHEAT CODE? MORE LIKE PETE CODE!
CAREFUL, GUYS!
WHOOOOOMPH
YO! A LITTLE HELP FOR YOUR HUMAN FRIENDS OVER HERE?
AH, YOUNG CASEY!
WHOA! SWEET SLAPSHOT!
WFFF-CRACK

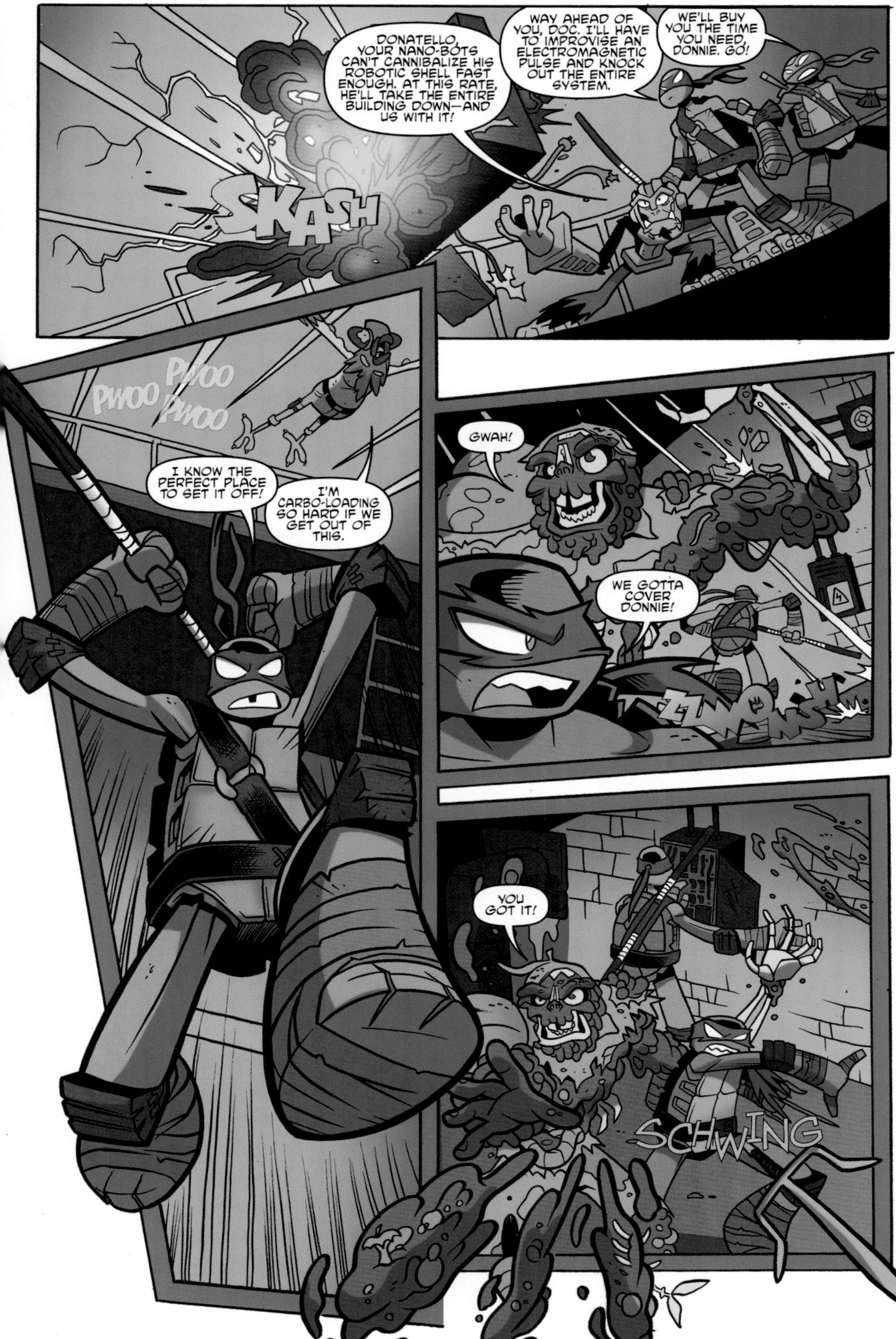
DONATELLO, YOUR NANO-BOTS CAN'T CANNIBALIZE HIS ROBOTIC SHELL FAST ENOUGH. AT THIS RATE, HE'LL TAKE THE ENTIRE BUILDING DOWN—AND US WITH IT!
WAY AHEAD OF YOU, DOC. I'LL HAVE TO IMPROVISE AN ELECTROMAGNETIC PULSE AND KNOCK OUT THE ENTIRE SYSTEM.
WE'LL BUY YOU THE TIME YOU NEED, DONNIE. GO!
SKASH
PWOO PWOO PWOO PWOO
I KNOW THE PERFECT PLACE TO SET IT OFF!
I'M CARBO-LOADING SO HARD IF WE GET OUT OF THIS.
GWAH!
WE GOTTA COVER DONNIE!
YOU GOT IT!
SCHWING

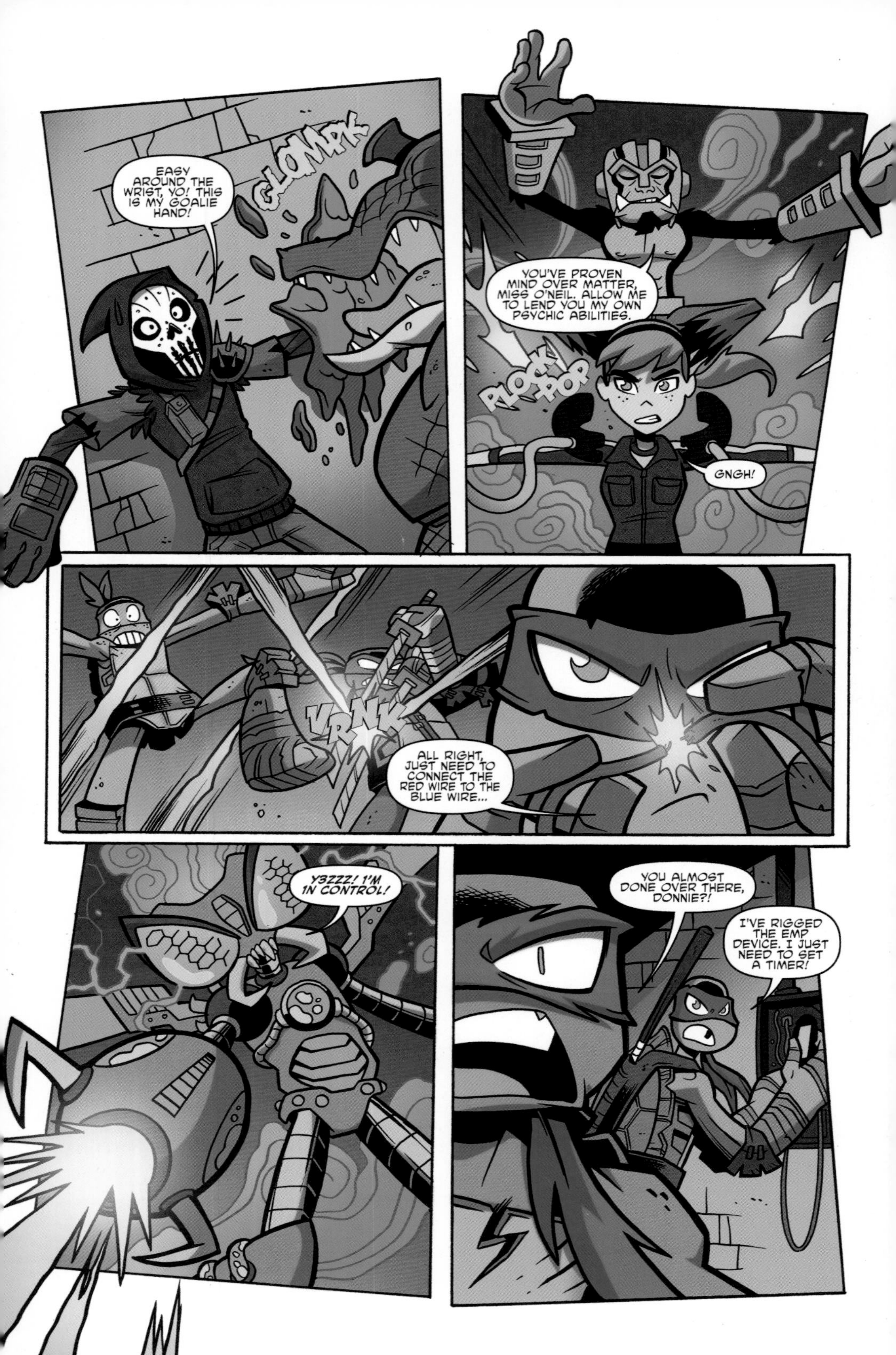
EASY AROUND THE WRIST, YO! THIS IS MY GOALIE HAND!
GLOMPK
YOU'VE PROVEN MIND OVER MATTER, MISS O'NEIL. ALLOW ME TO LEND YOU MY OWN PSYCHIC ABILITIES.
PLOCK POP
GNGH!
VRNK
ALL RIGHT, JUST NEED TO CONNECT THE RED WIRE TO THE BLUE WIRE...
Y3ZZZ! I'M 1N CONTROL!
YOU ALMOST DONE OVER THERE, DONNIE?!
I'VE RIGGED THE EMP DEVICE. I JUST NEED TO SET A TIMER!

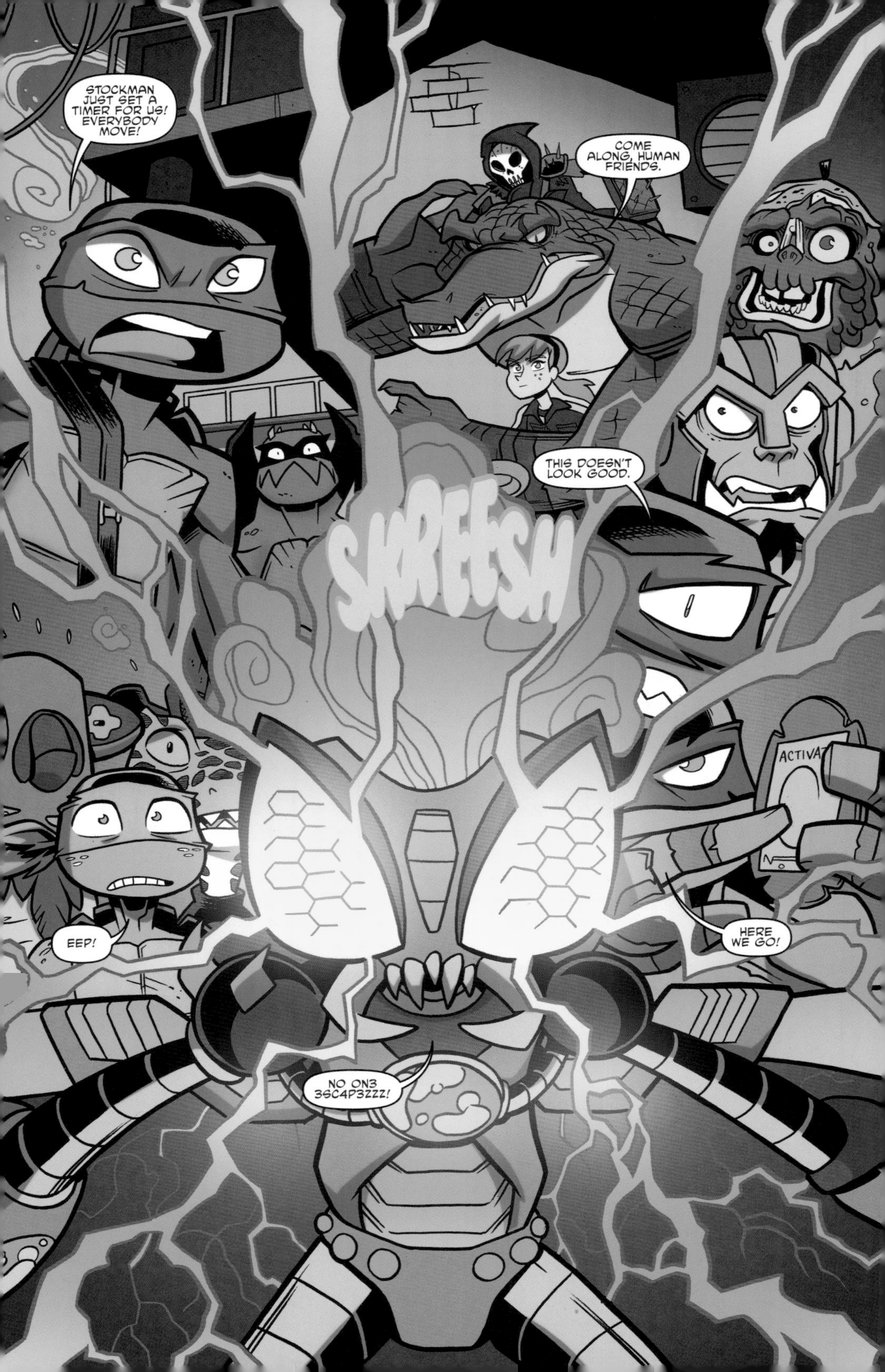
STOCKMAN JUST SET A TIMER FOR US! EVERYBODY MOVE!
COME ALONG, HUMAN FRIENDS.
THIS DOESN'T LOOK GOOD.
SKREESH
ACTIVAT
EEP!
HERE WE GO!
NO ON3 3SC4P3ZZZ!

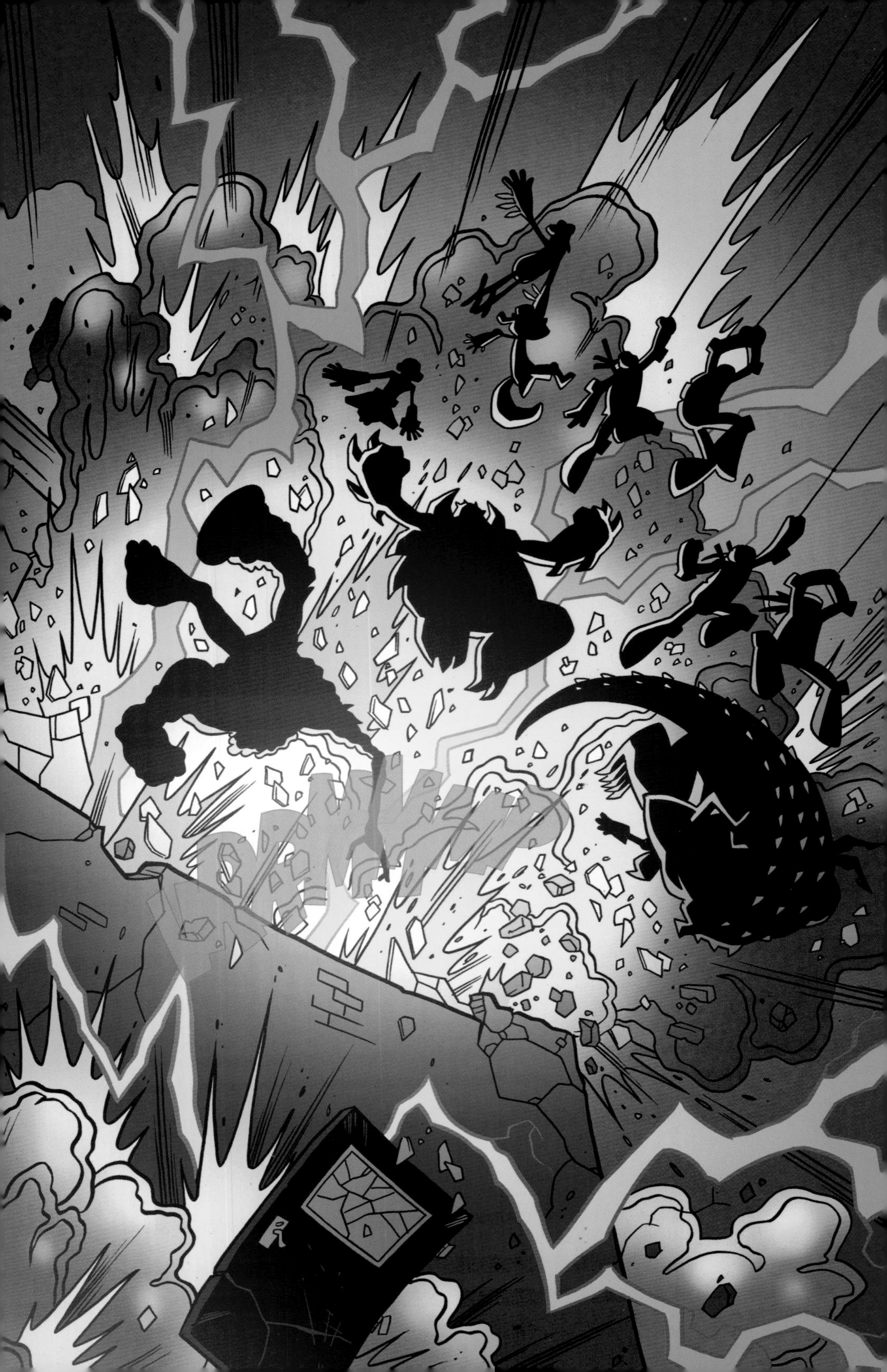

IS EVERYBODY ALL RIGHT?

HEADCOUNT LOOKS GOOD. WE MADE IT!

THE BUDDY SYSTEM WORKS!

THANKS, LEATHERBRO!

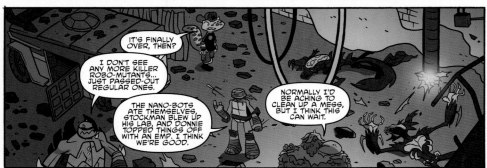

IT'S FINALLY OVER, THEN?

I DON'T SEE ANY MORE KILLER ROBO-MUTANTS... JUST PASSED-OUT REGULAR ONES.

THE NANO-BOTS ATE THEMSELVES, STOCKMAN BLEW UP HIS LAB, AND DONNIE TOPPED THINGS OFF WITH AN EMP. I THINK WE'RE GOOD.

NORMALLY I'D BE ACHING TO CLEAN UP A MESS, BUT I THINK THIS CAN WAIT.

STOKED TO HEAR ABOUT THE SCIENCE-Y STUFF, GUYS, BUT I DO BELIEVE WE COULD ALL DO WITH RESUMING THE *PIZZA PARTY*.

WITH THE EMP BLAST, I'M NOT SURE THE PARTY WAGON WILL EVEN START.

GREAT. LOOKS LIKE WE'RE PUSHING IT HOME.

NAH, RAPH. I GOT THIS.

GOOD THING CASEY JONES DOESN'T KNOW HOW ELECTRONICS WORK!

CHNG-CHNG-VHOOM

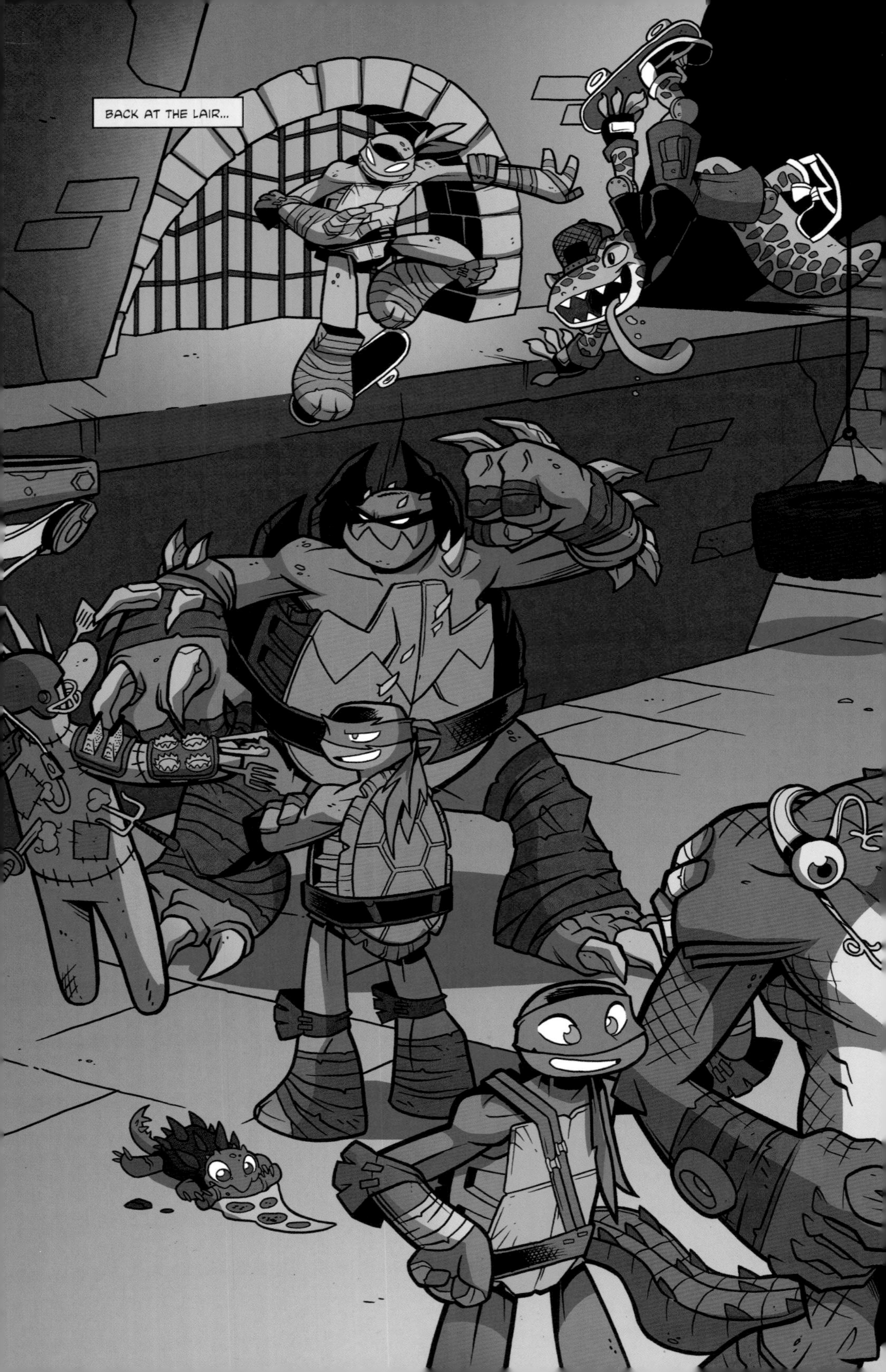
BACK AT THE LAIR...

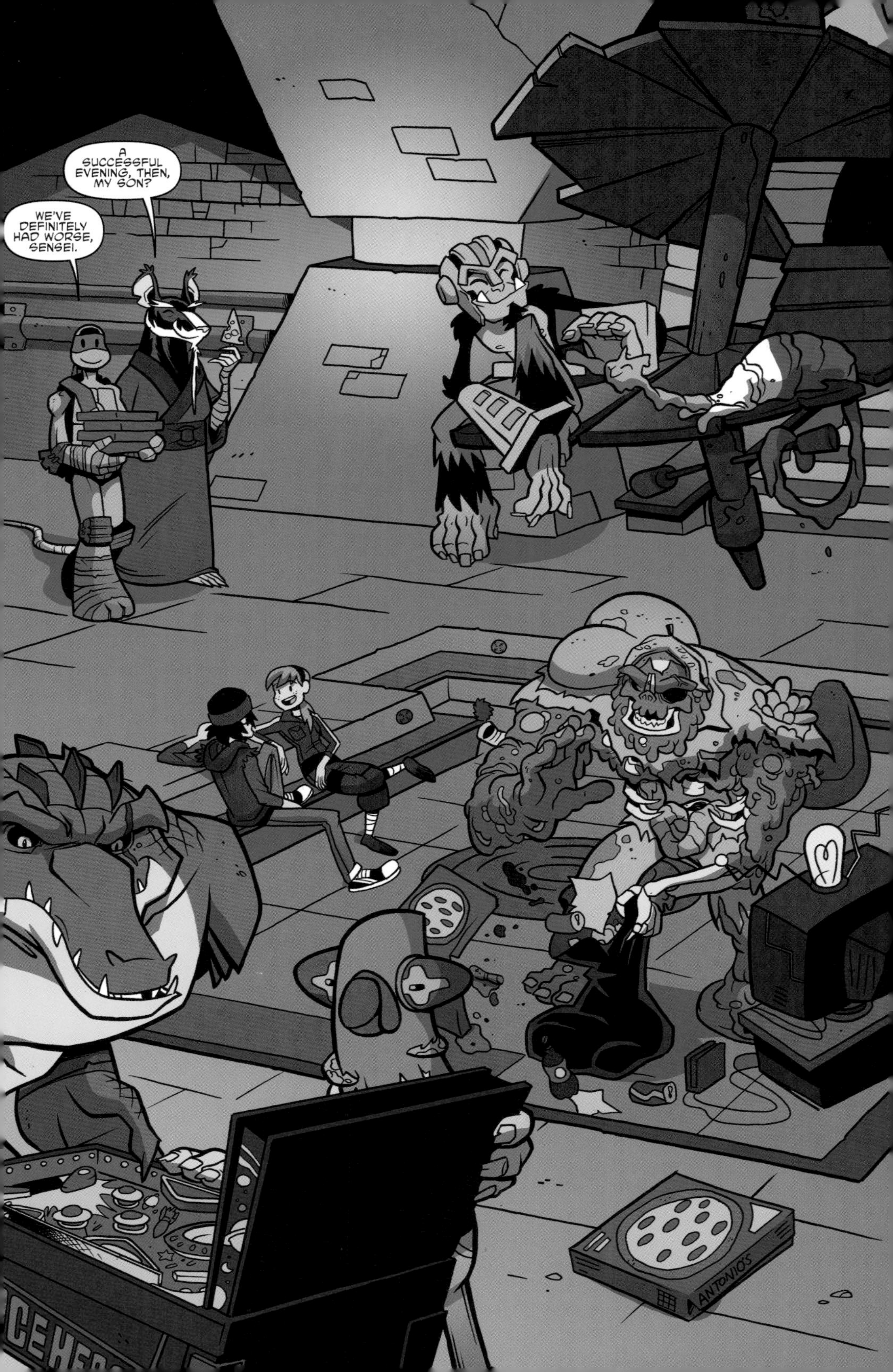
A SUCCESSFUL EVENING, THEN, MY SON?
WE'VE DEFINITELY HAD WORSE, SENSEI.
ANTONIOS

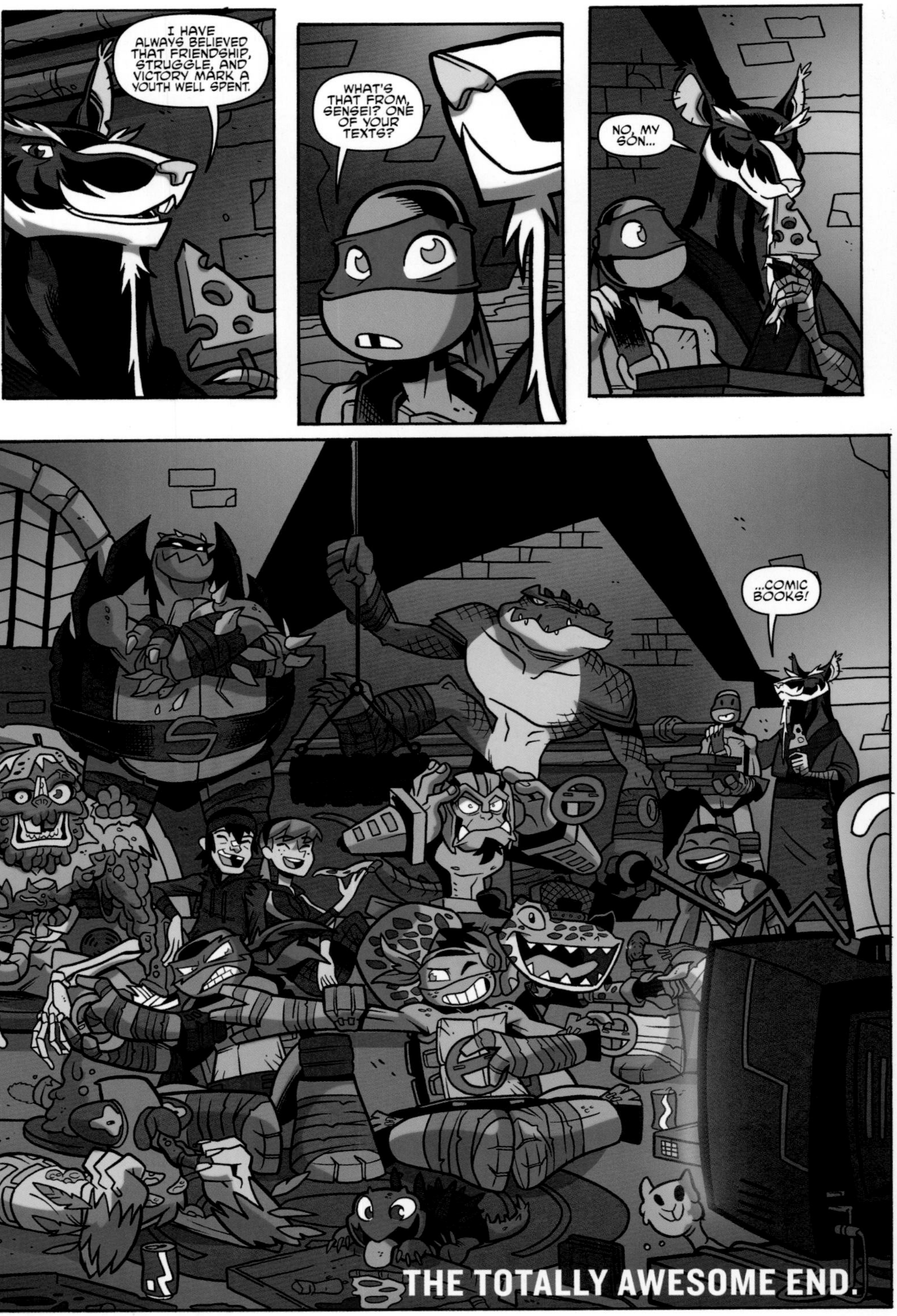
I HAVE ALWAYS BELIEVED THAT FRIENDSHIP, STRUGGLE, AND VICTORY MARK A YOUTH WELL SPENT.
WHAT'S THAT FROM, SENSEI? ONE OF YOUR TEXTS?
NO, MY SON...
...COMIC BOOKS!
THE TOTALLY AWESOME END.

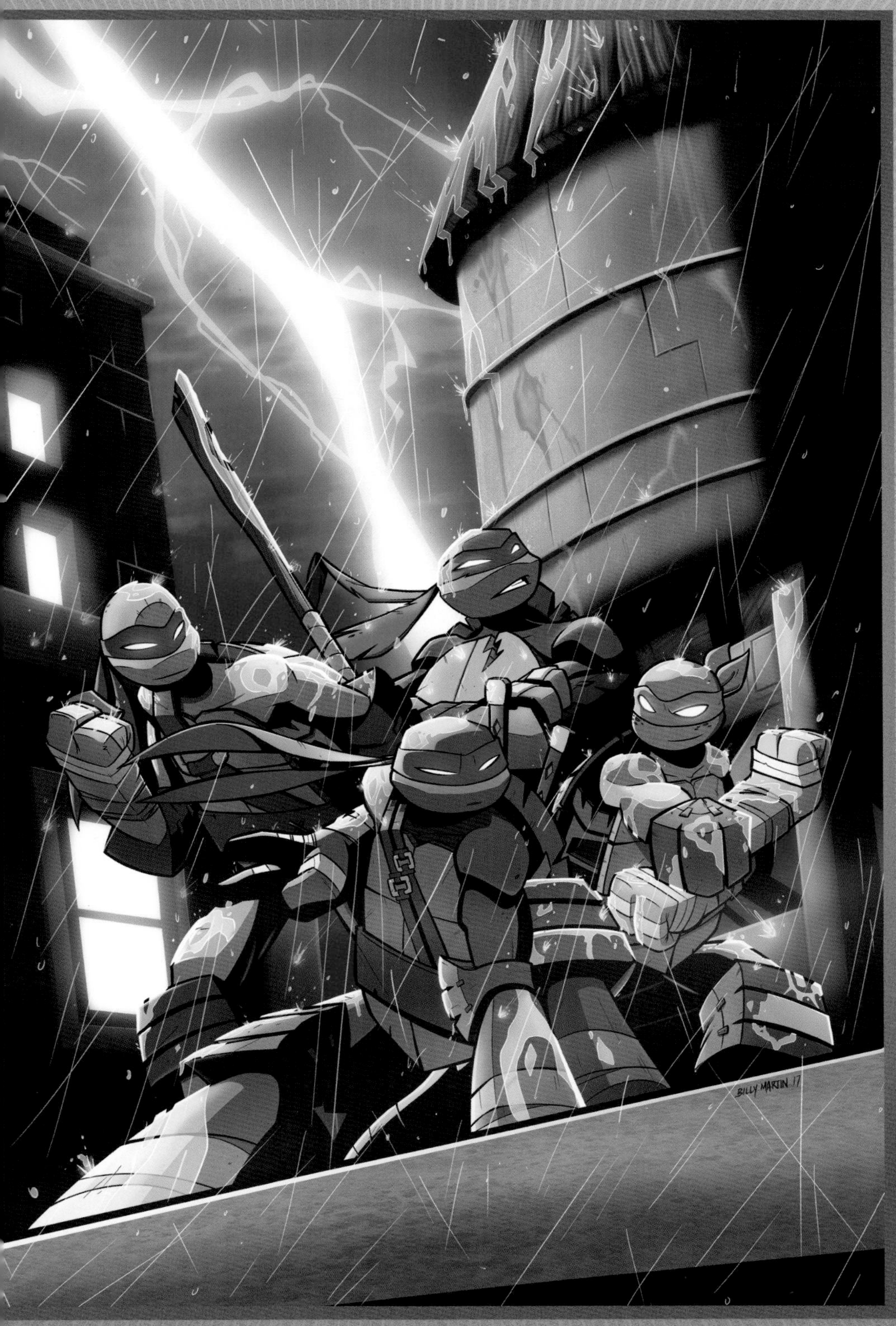
BILLY MARTIN '17

Artist: Billy Martin

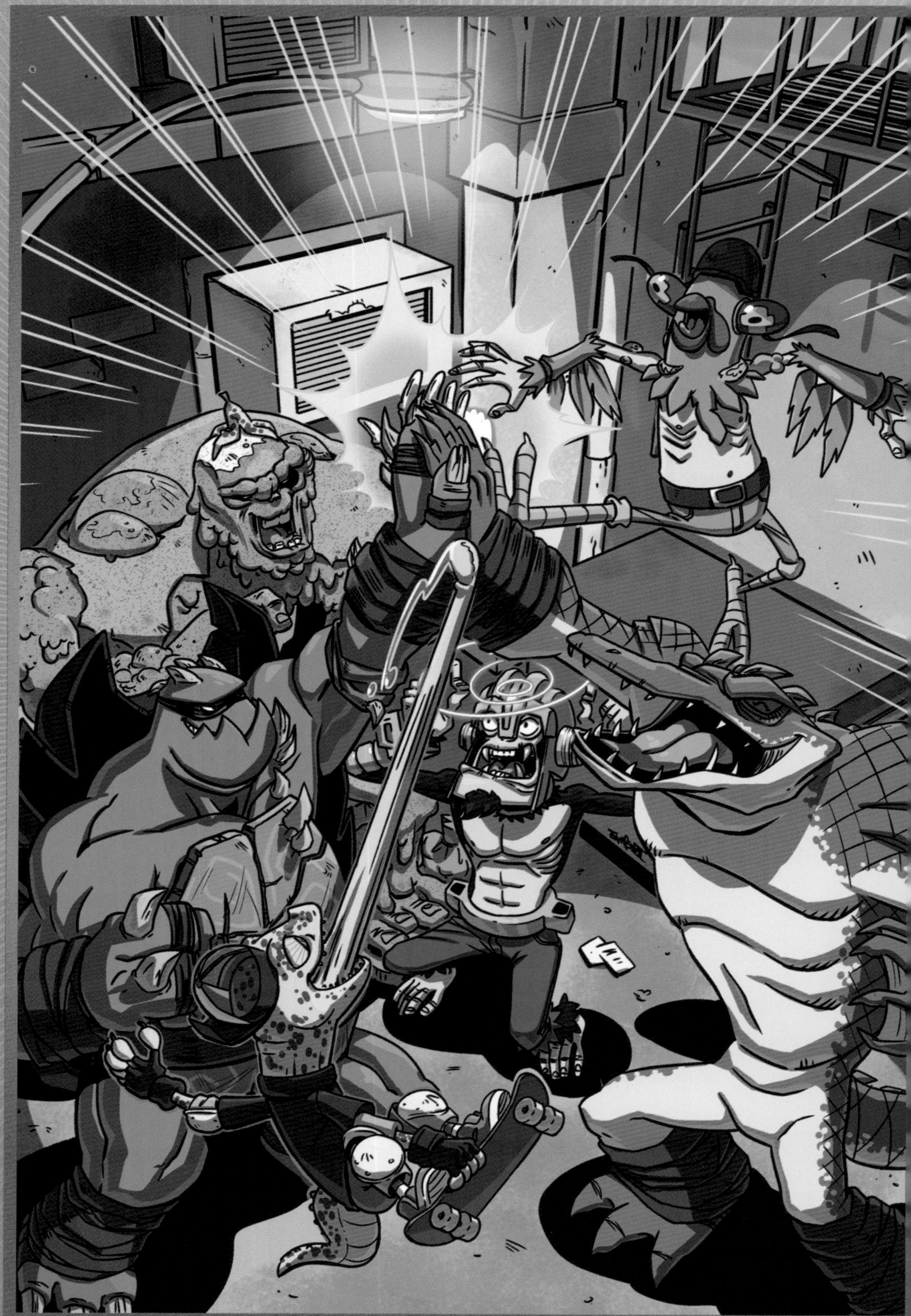

Artist: Ryan Jampole

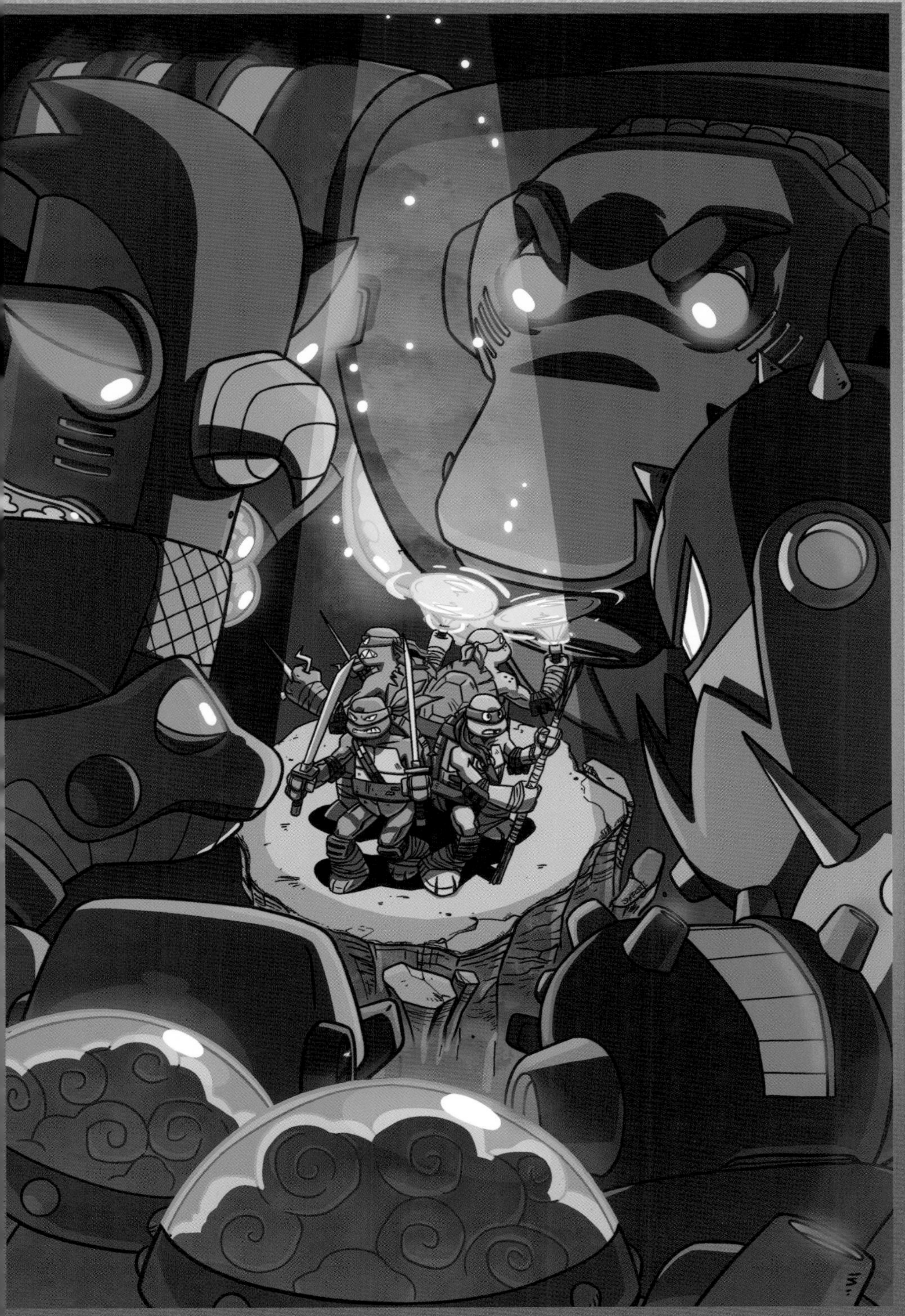

Artist: Ryan Jampole

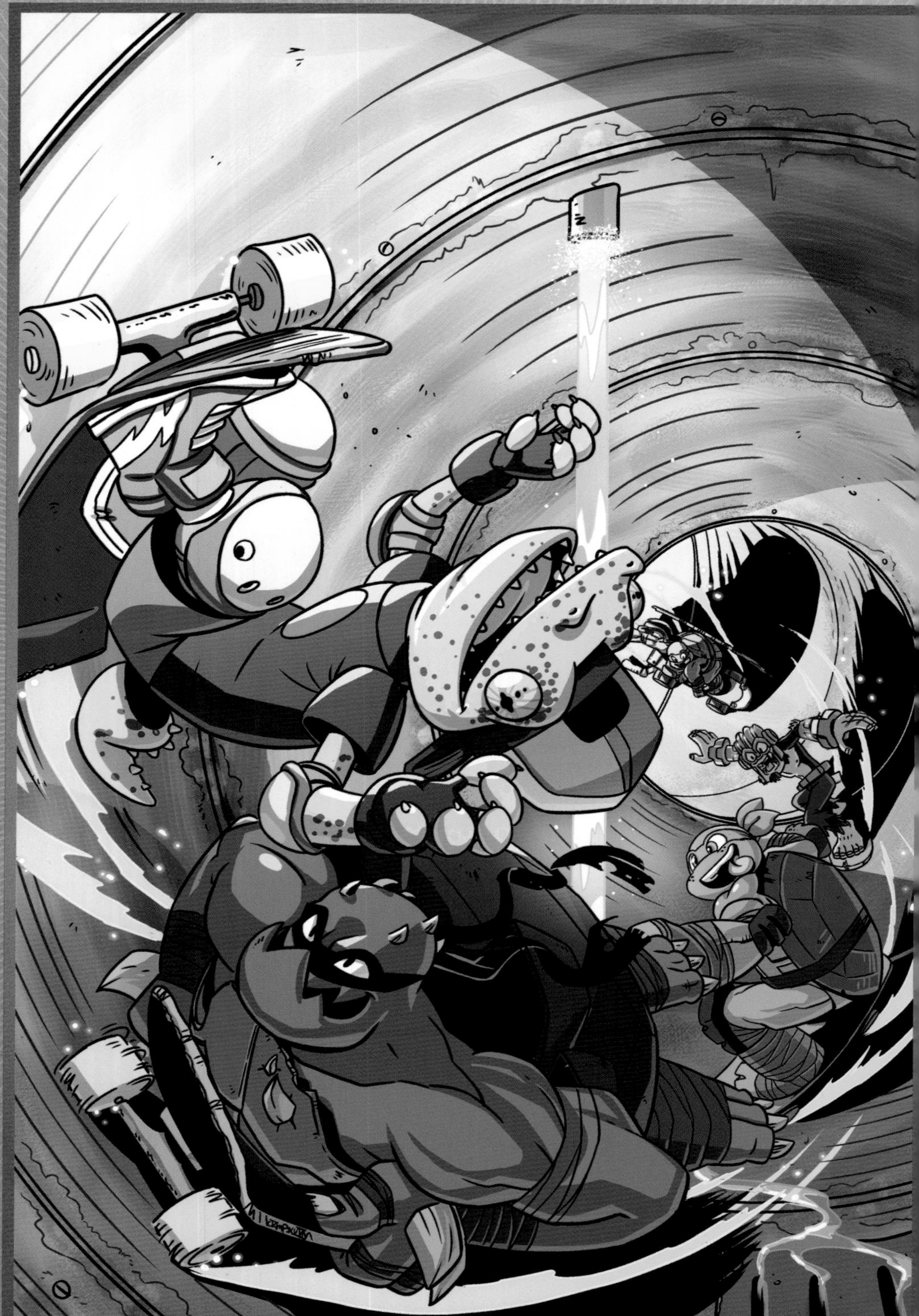

Artist: Ryan Jampole